CONQUER THE HILL

Book Two in the

Tony Simons Series

I0679635

Larry & Shirley Crandell

Publishers: Mcnally Robinson/Larry & Shirley Crandell

2019

ISBN: 9781772802870

Edited by: Kathryn Crandell and Garry & Brenda Boese

Cover Image by: VladimirGjorgiev/Shutterstock.com

"Do not go where the path may lead you, go instead where there is no path and leave a trail."

-    Ralph Waldo Emerson

Acknowledgement

Writing this book was harder than we thought it would be when we first began and more rewarding than we could ever have imagined when it was finished.

Shirley and I have pretty wild imaginations but my memories as to what might have happened almost forty years ago while in the military was a little thin. We not only wanted to grab the readers' interest so that they would continue to read our story, but also touch on other readers' memories and have them say "I think I remember doing that."

Research is everything in building a good story but nothing is better than getting a little help from a few hundred old and new friends that have a better memory than mine. One of these old friends stands out of the crowd and his recollection of that time gone by was invaluable to us in completing this adventure.

At this time we have to acknowledge and thank a blast from the past, Ken Fanjoy, AKA Mr. Handsome, for all his help in navigating the way through what I had long forgotten.

Last but not least I would like to acknowledge the Canadian Military for giving me the time of my life and friends I will never forget.

PROLOGUE

Tony thought he was prepared for what was to come. He was excited. He saw himself all decked out in his shiny new uniform with girls going crazy over him.

He knew it was going to be hard. It would be long hours and little sleep. He was ready for that; he wasn't ready for Sergeant McArthur.

"You are civilians in my eyes and I hate civilians. My mother was a civilian and I hate my mother."

Then Tony's nightmare came true and it was named Corporal John Thomas Willows. His eyes rolled as Corporal Willows bellowed "You will call me Corporal Willows and nothing else. I've been in this military since dirt was rocks. I will be your instructor in all things military for the next ten weeks. Right now you maggots are the shit on the bottom of my combat boot and I will try to scrape you off my boot every day you are here. I'm going to be as much fun for you as a heart attack, ladies. Is that clear?"

"Yes Corporal" and "yes sir" were their weak replies. Their response was met with a battle cry from Corporal Willows that could be heard through all four buses.

"When I talk to you meat sacks from now on, you will scream 'yes, Corporal Willows!' Is that clear?" The bus exploded "yes Corporal Willows!"

Tony was shitting a small brick, thinking about Willows in his face for the next ten weeks and it got even worse when Corporal Willows thought he had caught Tony staring at him and tore into him from the front of the bus.

"Why are you staring at me that way Simons? Do you love me Simons? Do you want to hold my hand in the shower you horrible little man? Stop eye-balling me!"

All Tony could think was "oh my god."

Chapter 1

Tony stood there frozen for a minute, watching his best friend Mark quickly fading away into the distance. Then he turned and entered the passenger car. He had never been on a train before and he found that it was larger than he had thought it would be. The seating was in groups of four or two. He was amazed at how quiet it was inside, as it picked up speed and charged down the tracks.

He looked into the compartment and found that the car was already quite full and a frown came over his face. Finally, he noted that about four rows down there were three empty seats. One next to a strange looking guy that Tony thought looked like a hippy. He had long hair covered by a beat up baseball cap that had seen too much sun, dark John Lennon glasses, a jean jacket and pants that had seen better days, and running shoes that were covered in paint, or what could have been dried concrete. He looked to be older than Tony, but what really stood out was that he sported one hell of a large mustache.

The stranger was sitting there, quietly smoking a cigarette as Tony entered the car and he seemed to be sizing Tony up. He caught Tony's eye and motioned for him to take the seat next to him. Tony moved in and sat down at the window seat. The two seats across from them were still empty. The stranger offered him a smoke, lit it and waited for Tony to take a drag.

"I noticed you on the platform," he said with a smile. "You hang with some pretty strange dudes there, Pilgrim." Tony nodded in agreement. The stranger then sat back and put his cigarette out in the ashtray and looked Tony in the eye. "My name is Keith; you can call me KG." To which Tony replied "my name is Tony, just Tony." He then turned back to the window and noticed that Port Nichols had faded away and the vast fruit lands of the Niagara Peninsula were filling his view. Fear welled up in his stomach and he could feel cold sweat starting to form around his neck. He was doing this; he was making a new start with nothing but questions in front of him.

Tony didn't realize that he had begun breathing harder and was starting to steam up the window, while at the same time creating a death-grip on the seat rest. He started to doubt himself as panic set in and then he heard a voice, barely understandable, coming from his left. "I swear to god I nev… mumble, mumble, mumble…in one place at one time." Tony snapped out of his self-made terrors and looked at the man sitting next to him.

Tony swore that the man had barely moved since he sat down but he could see his mustache moving, eyes peering through his Lennon glasses under the rim of the old ball cap. He repeated his observations again. "I have never seen so many homely women in one place at one time ever before. It hurts my eyes."

Tony was still coming out of his trance as he looked at Keith. "Are you talking to me? Did I hear you right?" Keith pushed up his glasses, took a deep breath and sighed. "Look around, Pilgrim, tell me what you see." "You want me to look around?" Tony answered quickly. He moved nothing but his eyes and volunteered no emotions as he took a look at the other people in the car. It was full, like he already knew, but now he could see what Keith was talking about.

There were around 20 guys wearing little stick-on nametags, drinking beers and loudly laughing at conversations that Tony could not hear. He guessed what the discussions might be about.

There were a few older couples travelling to who knows where that were unhappy with the goings on from these guys, but what could they do? Then Tony noticed what Keith had been talking about. The car contained about ten young ladies of varying sizes and descriptions in little groups or by themselves. Some were laughing behind magazines and pointing to some of the guys who were drinking, others were hiding in the corners with their sweaters buttoned right up, head down, hoping not to be noticed.

Tony decided to himself that these girls need not worry about their virtues, they were safe. "Holy Christ!" was all he could say as he gazed around the car.

Again his mustached friend's lips moved and wisdom came forth. "There is not enough booze on the train that I could drink to make these ugly females beautiful. I need alcohol now, beer is calling, are you coming?"

Tony suddenly realized just how thirsty he was. It had been some time since coffee at Liz's place that morning. "You lead and I'll follow" Tony said. "Do you know where the club car is?" "That's easy man" Keith said "just follow the crowd." They both got up to move forward when Keith looked back and told him they should leave their "shit" on the seats so they'd have one to come back to.

Tony dropped his backpack in the chair and Keith left his jean jacket. They moved forward to the next car only to find it full of little paper nametags. They moved on to the next car and found beer heaven.

As they entered the car Tony could smell hotdogs steaming from behind the bar. The small tables were occupied by an assortment of people who were having loud conversations as they drank and wolfed down food they had gotten from the bar.

As luck would have it, they found two seats at the bar and ordered two long-necks which they inhaled immediately and ordered two more. They started up mild conversation back and forth and Tony found himself fascinated with Keith's story of living outside of Saskatoon, Saskatchewan and working on a grain farm all his life. His dad had worked him hard from sunup until dusk but the farm was failing and Keith had to get away while he still could.

Tony's friend went on for some time without stopping. It was like he was unburdening himself and needed to speak. They talked about what was ahead for them and whether they could make it. They had to make it; they had no choice.

Basic Training was for all three elements, Army, Navy and Air Force. Both Keith and Tony would be entering the Air Force after it was completed.

The beers went down quicker and easier, and they made a drunken pact that they would have each other's backs while they were in recruit training and they would drag each other across the finish line.

While this was going on, Keith was noticing Tony more. Tall for his age, in shape no doubt, with an intense stare, like he was watching for trouble. Keith knew that his new friend had a story to tell but that would come later. He had talked enough for both of them for now.

Food! There must be food somewhere! Keith was starving. "We've got to eat Tony, and soon!" They looked at the wall menu and decided that they were not going to spend $8 on a tuna sandwich that was probably four days old and the hotdogs didn't look very appetizing. The beer was expensive enough. A light came on in Tony's clouded mind. Liz had made him roast beef sandwiches and she had thrown in some homemade cookies too!

Tony told Keith he had a veritable feast in his backpack and they were going to eat like kings! Keith's eyes lit up and he told Tony to lead on. They moved toward their car quickly. Tony could hardly wait.

Chapter 2

When they moved past a gaggle of grinning homely ladies, Tony heard Keith muttering again, under his "stache." Keith looked at him again and shrugged. "I told you Tony, we've been drinking all afternoon and they're still homely." Tony broke out laughing and was shaking his head as they turned a corner into their car.

Something was wrong. They moved down the aisle, and their minds lit up through the beer buzz. There were strangers sitting in their seats. Tony could see his backpack on the aisle floor getting kicked around as people passed. Keith could see what was happening and that Tony had gone silent and cold as a grave. The blood left his face and his jaw locked tight in a serious stare.

Keith tensed up in anticipation of what was going to happen. Tony moved quickly to his seating area and stopped directly in front of the sitting stranger. His buddies were behind Tony in the other seats, so they were looking at his ass. The stranger's hair and that of his posse of no-minds were cut down to the wood. The stranger was especially noticeable because his ears folded out like a pair of wings.

Mr. Football noticed Tony right away and was in the process of saying "what the fuck," when Tony calmly said "you shit birds are in our seats." Tony remembered that during his many bar fights he learned never to give his opponent a chance. Strike first, fast and finally.

Mr. Football was beaking off that these were his seats now and no hippy freaks were going to say different. He told Tony to fuck off or he and his friends were going to lay a beating on him.

Tony noted that the car had gone quiet and he could feel eyes on the group.

Keith had moved closer to the yappy friends of Mr. Football and Tony quickly looked back to see a nasty look come over his friend's face.

Mr. Football's friends started to rant "break his face Kevin, make him bleed." Mr. Football tried to raise himself up out of the chair by grabbing Tony by the shoulder. That was his mistake. Tony went black and found himself in the Franklin bar that fateful night that the drunk grabbed him from behind and said "you're Dick's kid, aren't you?"

Mr. Football was on the receiving end of two hard punches to the face and a mean elbow to the side of his head, splitting open one of his large ears and turning his jacket even redder than it was before.

Tony could hear gasps and a scream coming from the corner of the car.

Keith moved in and pounded the posse around their heads with no mercy. One of them even started to cry. It was over before it really got started and Keith had to pull Tony off Mr. Football to bring him back from wherever he was.

"It's over man," Keith said, "he's had enough." Tony blinked twice and found himself back in the train car with his hands gripping Mr. Football's coat. He got his breathing back under control and looked at him darkly. "Did you toss my shit on the floor, along with my friend's coat?" Mr. Football was already regretting his answer, but told Tony they had indeed put their stuff on the floor because they wanted the seats.

"Now I want something," Tony said, and yanked the man to his feet. "Pick up my stuff and hand it to me right now." Mr. Football bent down and picked up the guys' belongings and handed them to him. "I'm sorry, man, I'm really sorry." Mr. Football could not believe the beating that he and his friends had just received over a seat. He tried to move away from Tony but was stopped in his tracks. Tony was looking at the paper nametag on Mr. Football's jacket. "Kevin Fielding" was typed on it. Tony looked at the tag and then at Kevin. "Please tell me you stole that tag from some scared little kid that you trapped in the washroom." Kevin said "hell no," he and his buddies were joining the military and going into the army.

Tony shook his head and looked at Keith, "do you believe this piece of shit?" and looked back at Kevin. Tony reached into his pocket and pulled his tag out and stuck it on his jacket. He turned to see Keith doing the same and noticed that his name tag said "Keith Stoddard."

The blood drained from Kevin Fielding's face as he looked at the tag. Tony let go of Fielding's coat and smiled at him in an evil way. "I'll see you later asshole, now get out of my face."

Mr. Football and his buddies quickly and quietly moved down the aisle and out of the car.

Tony and Keith sat down in their seats and took a few deep breaths and just like nothing happened, Tony opened up "like I was saying buds my friend Liz made these great roast beef sandwiches for the trip, and I know there'll be plenty. I know you're going to love them."

The car had quieted down again. Tony opened his backpack and was immediately confronted with the aroma of the roast beef. It took him back to Liz's kitchen and the great food he had had there. He gave Keith a huge sandwich and took one for himself. As promised, they were delicious. The boys sat in silence as they ate and about half way through, Keith stopped and looked at his new-found friend. "You're kind of touchy about some things aren't you?" Tony just nodded and continued to eat his sandwich.

The rest of the trip to Trenton was uneventful and the guys had time to sit back, relax and have a smoke. The intercom clicked on and an even-voiced person announced that Trenton station was five minutes out and passengers should ready themselves for arrival.

Chapter 3

According to Tony's Travel Orders they would be taking a bus to the AMU Trenton which was across town and would take about an hour.

Once they arrived, they stepped out of the train and walked out of the terminal to find four military buses waiting for them right at the front door.

The military drivers were waving them in and they loaded quickly for the next leg of the trip. The driver didn't say much except that they were headed for Canadian Forces Base Trenton/8 Wing, located on the east side of town. This facility was the hub of the Royal Canadian Forces Transport and Search and Rescue Operations. It was the town of Trenton's main employer and a big deal. The driver warned them against getting into trouble while they were there.

The ride was uneventful, but the guys had their faces pressed up against the window so as to take everything in and not miss seeing the upcoming Base. They didn't have to wait long before they arrived at the AMU. Tony asked the driver what the term "AMU" meant and the driver shook his head in disbelief and said that it stood for "Air Movements Unit." "Just keep your eyes open and your mouths closed, recruits, and I'll get you to where you need to be."

The bus stopped in front of the main gate and Tony started to see uniforms, lots of uniforms and armed men wearing military police bands on their arms. The front of the AMU was huge and Tony knew that he was about to enter a new world. The world of the military waited just beyond the gate.

Everybody was rubber-necking everywhere, but failed to hear the door open and a tall, intense looking person in full dress uniform stepped in. "Listen up, you lost lambs in civilian clothing! My name is Sergeant William McArthur, you'll address me as Sergeant McArthur at all times, and nothing else. When I speak to you, your eyes will click and your ears will pick up everything I'm going to say, because I'm only going to say it once. Let's get something straight right from the beginning of your adventure at my AMU. You are civilians in my eyes, and I hate civilians. My mother is a civilian and I hate my mother. Before you lost Marys move from your seats, you will look in your Travel Orders and remove your Leave Pass. You will present this paper to the security personnel at the gate before entering into the complex. When you leave the bus you will form three lines in front of the entry points and wait for your name to be called. You are to keep your belongings with you at all times. If you talk in line or gawk around I will take your skin! Once you clear security, enter the building and turn right. There is a designated area set out for you. Do not leave this area, I will be there momentarily. Do you understand the instructions I have given you?"

There was a bunch of low OK's and a few "Sergeants," but they lit up quickly when Sergeant McArthur breathed fire and his face went bright red. "What did you call me, you maggots?" "Yes, Sergeant McArthur" came a loud booming answer.

The recruits moved from the bus in great haste and the Sergeant was there to make sure they did. They formed up in front of the gates with their Leave Passes in hand, waiting for their name to be called. Tony caught Keith looking at him and rolling his eyes in disbelief.

Suddenly, there was a big commotion in front of one of the lines. It was Tony's line. An MP (Military Policeman) was looking at a recruit. "Is this your Leave Pass Recruit? What's your name, recruit? Did I call your name?" "Yes," the recruit answered. "I am a Corporal, Recruit and you will answer, Yes Corporal! Do you understand?" "Yes Corporal," the answer came in a shaky voice. "What is your

SIN number Recruit Cummings?" A blank stare came over the recruit and you could see him melt under the questioning. "Your SIN number Cummings, do you know your SIN number? Have you even looked at your Leave Pass? Can you read, Cummings? Your SIN number is right there in the upper left hand corner. Read the number to me Cummings, so that I will know that you truly went to school."

This humiliation was not lost on Tony's group and they all quickly looked at their passes. It was their "Social Insurance Number." Tony shook his head and thought to himself "more damn code to learn." He passed through security with little trouble and hurried into the AMU.

Tony was taken aback by the beautiful vast room that boomed with activity, military activity. Large carved pictures of wilderness scenes and aircraft adorned the walls, along with statues of uniformed personnel, including the RCMP. Awards of one type or another could be seen in every corner and nearly everything was made of oak. Even the main arrivals' and departures' desk area was a beautiful blond oak. The far wall was a huge window with massive sliding doors leading to the runway that greeted military people coming or going from somewhere.

The guys could look at this all day and not get tired for this was their world now.

They moved into the holding area and saw long lines of benches and seats that were marked "Recruit Holding." Before they knew it, Sergeant McArthur was in front of the group again. "Did you Marys look around outside to make sure you all got in? Nobody left behind?" They knew better this time, a loud "No missing recruits Sergeant McArthur!" came from the group.

"A little birdie tells me, you lambs didn't even know your SIN number yet! What is the military hiring these days? It's sad, very sad." The Sergeant became ramrod straight and bellowed out loud, "Cummings! Where are you Cummings? Come forward and stand in front of me. The MP says that maybe you can't read Cummings; is this true?" Cummings was dying inside, as he stood up.

"Just for giving me a laugh today, Cummings, you now have volunteered to help me during your stay here at this fine AMU. First up ladies, I've been informed that your flight to Halifax has been delayed for three hours due to weather. This means we get to feed you so you don't complain to your congressmen. Cummings!" he boomed. "Get a head count back to me in five minutes so we can order dinner for our new fighting men. If anybody goes missing after the head count it will mean that I get to hang Recruit Cummings on the fence and get a new volunteer."

The recruit was gone in a flash and returned to the Sergeant in under three minutes. "There are 80 men Sergeant McArthur." The Sergeant shook his head and said he would make supper happen and that his new volunteer was to be his eyes and ears while he was away.

Cummings was visibly shaken by this encounter with Sergeant McArthur.

Meanwhile Tony and Keith could see a lot from the holding area and before they knew it the Sergeant had returned with two Privates rolling in 80 box lunches for the recruits.

A box lunch is a military staple wherever you are. They usually contained two sandwiches, fruit, cookies and a drink of some kind. The recruits gobbled the gourmet delights away in no time.

Cummings was tasked with the cleaning of the area.

Before the Sergeant left he also tasked his volunteer with setting up bathroom breaks and groups to tour the AMU in order to keep them occupied.

The time went quickly and finally the guys saw their flight number come up on the board, arriving in 15 minutes. The group was reassembled in the holding area and warned again to keep their personal kit with them at all times.

Tony was getting excited again. Another first, he had never been on a plane. He noted that today there were a lot of firsts.

Chapter 4

The giant plane rolled up to the big doors and stopped only feet from the building. The intercom announced that Flight 712 to Halifax would be boarding by rows and personnel could proceed to the plane when their rows were called. Tony and Keith would be sitting together and as they got to the top of the stairs leading into the airplane, they looked back and saw Sergeant McArthur chewing out Recruit Cummings one more time, because he had left his coat behind!

The guys looked at one another and said that they would never forget that crazy old Sergeant and turned to enter the plane.

To Tony, it was huge inside and looked as long as a football field. He thought that there was no way in hell that this thing was going to get off the ground! Tony thought for sure they were going to crash and burn at the end of the runway.

The plane was quiet inside and Tony and Keith found their seats with no problem. Keith was sitting in the aisle seat and Tony had the window. Tony looked out the window to see the giant wing and thought "no way."

The monster was filling up quickly and Tony could see that most there were recruits. The "fasten seatbelt" sign came on and Tony wasn't sure at all how to use the buckle. He finally got the belt snapped shut but pulled the belt so tight he couldn't breathe. Then the engines came to life and Tony felt the power move throughout the plane. He started to hyperventilate and fogged up the window again. More power was added to the engines and the plane started to move into the night.

Tony was as tense as a scared cat as he looked out the window, and heard Keith beside him say, as calm as he could, "I'm going to take a guess at this, but you haven't flown before, have you?" Tony looked at him and said "what gave it away, smart ass?" Keith snickered and said "don't worry buddy, if this baby goes down, you'll be dead before you hit the ground. Now get your hand off my knee, I'm starting to lose circulation in my leg."

Tony felt the dragon come to life and scream down the runway. The power pushed him back in his seat. The nose came up and it was over. Tony was in the air!

The pressure returned to the cabin as the bird climbed into the night. Tony looked out the window as the lights on the ground faded away. The seatbelt sign went out and along with that the "smoking" sign came on.

Tony looked over to see Keith smirking at him. Tony looked back at him and Keith said "admit it buddy, it was great, wasn't it?" Tony had to agree, flying was a head rush.

The flight would take about two hours, putting them into Halifax at midnight and from there would be another two-hour bus ride to their new home. The guys lit up a smoke and were served coffee from a really nice-looking stewardess.

The boys had a light supper later and the flight was over before they knew it. The Captain came over the intercom and said that they were coming into Halifax. The "seatbelt" sign was on and the "smoking" sign was off.

Tony was very much aware that they were coming down. He looked out the window to see the lights of the city coming into view. Down, down they came until the airfield runway came up to touch the plane's wheels. They were on the ground and the monster was slowing down. Brakes were applied and the aircraft came to a halt in front of the AMU in Halifax, Nova Scotia.

Tony and Keith looked at each other and gave each other a high five, two hours to go. Keith had looked at his watch; it was 2:15 a.m. Saturday. Tony told Keith it looked cold as hell outside and he was right. The doors opened and the recruits were treated to a good old-fashioned Halifax blizzard. Dark and cold, the recruits ran into the AMU to escape the wind and the snow.

All in, the doors finally closed and they were greeted by another booming voice coming from the doorway, leading to the parking lot. "Recruits!" he yelled. "Gather your kit, and board the buses just outside the door. We've got a way to go, and you lot are late!"

Tony and Keith got on the first bus out the door, which they found out later was driven by a Corporal Flint. When his bus was full, Corporal Flint stood up and welcomed them to the "Fax." The Corporal was from Nova Scotia and had been posted to Cornwallis, to the Transport Division. "I just got my ass ripped off by a pissed off Sergeant because you ladies are going to be late, and he wanted to know why. He was not a happy man. It's a good thing for you, that you won't be meeting him until Monday, so he'll have time to cool down."

Keith could hear Tony saying "Jesus Christ, he's blaming us for the bad weather!"

Corporal Flint went on to say that the run would be about two hours, weather permitting. "If you can sleep, this would be a good time to do it, because you lambs will be missing a shit-load of sleep over the next eleven weeks."

The guys settled back in the dark and closed their eyes.

"You're home little darlings!" Corporal Flint's voice boomed. Tony couldn't believe it. There in front of them, were the gates of CFB Cornwallis!

All four buses stopped and were waiting for something. The recruits didn't know why they were stopped so they were looking around, and talking amongst themselves. They saw the lights of the bus behind them come on, and someone entering. They missed their own surprise coming through their door in the dark. The lights came on and there stood a serious-looking, well-dressed Corporal with his cap pulled straight down on his near bald head. You could only just see his eyes, and the only other thing you could see in the dim light was his scowl and no-nonsense stare.

"My name is Corporal John Thomas Willows. You will call me Corporal Willows and nothing else. I have been in the military since dirt was rocks. I will be your instructor in all things military over the next eleven weeks. Right now you maggots are the shit on the bottom of my combat boot and I will try to scrape you off my boot every day you are here. I'm going to be as much fun for you as a heart attack, ladies. Is that clear?"

"Yes Corporal" and "yes sir" was their weak answers. The response was met with a battle cry from Corporal Willows which could be heard throughout all the buses. "When I talk to you meat-sacks from now on, you will scream 'yes Corporal Willows,' is that clear?"

The bus exploded "yes Corporal Willows!"

Tony was shitting a small brick, thinking about Willows in his face for the next ten weeks. It got even worse when Willows thought he had caught Tony staring at him too long and tore into him from the front of the bus.

"Why are you staring at me, Simons? Do you love me Simons? Do you want to hold my hand in the shower, you horrible little man? Stop eye balling me!"

All Tony could think was "oh my god."

Willows then stared at the driver and said "let's get this shit-show going."

Chapter 5

The buses entered the camp and made their way down a narrow, snow-covered road, lit by old-street lamps that Tony figured were from the 30's. They hardly gave off any light at all in the blowing snow, but Willows had a destination and the driver had done this before.

At the end of the street, the buses stopped at a large building with a round sloping roof. Tony would later know this building very well. It was a large Quonset hut the size of two football fields that they would later know to be the Drill Hall and Graduation Parade Square. All they had to do was survive Corporal Willows.

Willows stood up and looked down the aisle, "ok you meat sacks, we're going to have a look at what you brought with you."

Keith looked at Tony and quietly said "what the hell does he mean?" Tony smirked and said "he wants to see your junk, man." Raised eyeballs returned his gaze.

"Listen up you Marys. You will move quickly and quietly into the building, because I'm freezing my arse off out here. Line up on the yellow line facing the Base Crest on the wall. Now hear me clearly, you will not step over the line until you are ordered to do so and you will place your kit in front of the line, open for inspection. No talking, eyes front always! Now move!"

The bus broke out into activity as men and bags moved into the Hall. Tony didn't know what was coming next, but he was sure he wasn't going to like it. Willows liked his job way too much. When everybody was lined up, facing forward, the instructors came out in front of the gaggle and began to speak all at once to each of their groups.

Tony and Keith had to concentrate on what Willows was saying, or it would be lost in the thunder. "This is a personal kit inspection and drug declaration girls, and your only chance to hand over shit that doesn't belong here or is illegal. The instructors are going to leave the Hall for five minutes. During that time there will be an amnesty and anything you hand over or put in the bins you see in front of you will not be charged against you. This material will be removed with no questions asked. After the five minute amnesty, we will return and ask you for a declaration stating that you have no illegal weapons or drugs in your possession. We warn you ladies, if after the declaration we find anything that should not be there, you will wish you had never been born. Is that clear? Let me hear you meat sacks!" The roar went up "yes, Corporal Willows!"

"We are going to leave you now recruits. Make the right decisions, you have five minutes." Then they left.

The Hall was quiet, not a word was heard. Eyes stared straight ahead. A minute or so went by and still dead silence. Then Tony started to hear movement from his right side but couldn't see anyone until they came into view. Up to the bins the man went and dropped in a big knife.

Tony's mind was racing. How many of these guys were carrying weapons? More people began moving toward the bins. Tony saw more knives and a few small handguns, brass knuckles and even some numb chucks. Tony was shaking his head. How the hell did these guys get these weapons through security? There was also a lot of action around the drug bin. All Tony could think was "Holy Shit."

Five minutes went by quickly and the instructors came back in and began the declarations. Each man was asked if he had anything dangerous or illegal on his person. It was simply a yes or no answer.

"Open your kit in front of you recruits."

After a quick look in their kit bags, the instructors ordered them to close their kit bags and stand at attention. This went on for the better part of an hour but eventually the task was done.

Willows came to the front of his group and ordered them to stand at attention, eyes front. This order was repeated by the other three instructors to their charges. Then from somewhere behind them they could hear a door opening, a rustling and then heavy panting. Tony thought the sound was that of a dog? Could it be? Tony had been involved in situations where the police were using dogs to look for drugs.

Suddenly everyone was aware of a Military Police Officer and a dog positioned at either end of the kit line! Tony's heart pounded in his chest like never before. He knew he didn't have anything but he was still petrified. He had seen some of the stuff the other guys had put in the bins and was not sure if it all made it there. He wanted to look around so bad but thought better of it; so he listened.

He became aware of the dogs and their handlers moving down the line to the left and right of him. He knew the dogs were working the line and he prayed it would be over soon. He thought that even if most were not guilty of anything the instructors would be only too happy to use the opportunity as a teaching tool.

At that moment fate stepped in, the dog to the left stopped and sat down in front of a recruit that was staring into nothing. His instructor came forward and ordered him to his knees, then said "hands over your head, Recruit and lock your fingers together." The MP proceeded to open the recruit's kit bag, and the dog immediately found two bags of cocaine. The MP moved behind the recruit and handcuffs were applied. "You're under arrest for drug possession. Stand up and move forward."

The recruit and his possessions were removed from the building.

The silence was deafening but the inspection continued. Tony could see that it was just about over. Then two over from Tony's right he saw a recruit step forward. The MP immediately brought the dog over, told the recruit to open his kit bag, step back, kneel and put his hands behind his back. Again, the dog sniffed the kit bag and pulled out a rolled sock containing a baggy of cocaine. The recruit was arrested and also removed.

After the dogs had completed their search, the MPs left the building.

Willows came to the front of his group, and in a cold, even-toned voice, warned them "if I ever catch you lying again, I will personally march you to cells and slam the door.

He then ordered them to pick up their bags and face the door. This reminded Tony of prison movies he had seen and Willows was the guard.

"Ok you little darlings file out and get on the bus. It's time to go home and put you lambs to bed."

Chapter 6

The bus quickly filled. No one wanted to be last. They piled in and Corporal Willows entered and instructed the driver to proceed to building 34-7, St Croix Block. They drove slowly away from the Hall with only the old lights to show them the way into the depths of the training centre. They passed row upon row of strange looking buildings shaped like H's that appeared out of the dark through the snow storm, until they rolled up to one and stopped.

Through the falling snow and with only one outside light to guide them, the number 34-7 could be seen. They were finally home!

The other three buses stopped behind them and Tony could imagine the guys in them were thinking the same thing he was, "Alcatraz."

Willows stood up and addressed his charges. "Leave the bus quietly and move into the block single file. Go through the small office and through the double doors and move into the main living area. When everyone is in; last man closes the door. Watch your step leaving the bus ladies; I don't want to lose any of you before the real fun starts."

Tony checked his watch; it was 05:30 on Saturday morning. "Move in and find a cot, you'll be assigned a permanent sleeping area in the morning. For now you just have to make do. I'll see you in an hour and a half, keep it quiet and do not leave this block."

With that he was gone. It was time to find a cot and look around. Everyone was just too keyed up to think of sleep. Tony hadn't talked to Keith in quite awhile. They found cots next to each other and jabbered on like they hadn't seen each other in months.

Keith said "do you believe that asshole? What is his story? That man's got a god complex." Tony replied "I've died and gone to hell. Did you see those dogs? Did those guys actually think they could bring stuff in here? Do you think they're in jail?" Keith shook his head, yes. "They're gone man."

They walked around the complex like the other recruits and realized that the building was indeed a double H connected by a corridor that housed washrooms, showers, sinks and laundry rooms that contained ironing boards and work stations. This was a big area that they would find out soon, they had to clean every day.

It was "getting to know you time" in the barracks seeing that it was 6:30 in the morning and Corporal Willows would be showing up at any minute to continue his "Welcome to Hell" speech.

The guys from Tony's bus massed in the laundry area and introduced each other while shaking hands and discussing the Drill Hall inquisition of a few hours previous. They all agreed that Willows was going to be a real fucker and they were going to have to watch each other around him. Tony was taking this all in and this was the first time he heard the word "we" since this adventure began.

The door in the main area opened then and Corporal Willows entered and stood right in the middle of the floor. "Get your asses in gear and coats on, it's time for brekky, and we wouldn't want to be late. The cooks have been up all night slaving for you and about five hundred other souls and we wouldn't want to disappoint them. You've got one minute to get outside and form up in three lines facing the barracks. No talking, look straight ahead, don't move or your ass is mine."

Tony and Keith moved outside quickly and got into line with the rest of the group. The other three groups from the H block were formed up in similar fashion and ready to move.

"When I give you herd the order to come to attention, you'll straighten up, look forward and don't move. Attention!" Willows bellowed.

Tony went rigid and lifted himself into the air. Willows yelled again "when I say left turn, you'll turn smartly to the left and bring your left foot up and down in one motion. Left turn!" he called. Twenty guys moved like twenty guys. "What a shit show" was all they heard as the snow continued to fall.

Corporal Willows was in his element. He gave the command "By the left quick march! Listen to my call ladies as we begin to move. Left, right; left, right; left, right; left. Try not to embarrass us too much on the way down to chow, you horrible herd. Try to listen to my words when I say left, your left foot should be hitting the ground. That way everyone is in step."

Tony was listening and getting into it. He was marching, really marching!

They moved in a gaggle down the road with the rest of the recruits, down the road to the Mess Hall. This building was just for recruits and not the Base population.

Willows called "halt" and it sounded like, well it was hard to explain. "Single file from the left ladies in the door, hang up your coats and remember where you left them. Move into line with the rest of the men and move forward to the serving tables. Do not talk unless you are asked a question by the kitchen staff. Remember, what you take, you eat. Move now!"

Tony moved into the building quickly and got into line. He could smell bacon and ham and imagined how well he was going to eat. He was starving. While moving forward in line he heard whispers from other men already eating. He heard words like "fresh meat, new virgins," and other such verbiage could be heard from the other tables.

Tony was painfully aware that they were the only guys there in civilian clothes and everybody knew it. He tried to put his head down and melt away. Breakfast was a disaster. Everything tasted like gruel and what passed for bacon was never identified.

It was a long half hour, but they got through it and back to the barracks with minimal calamity. There was only one incident on the way back. It was still snowing and one of the recruits had the wrong shoes on and fell down in the middle of the gaggle of men, bringing down four others. This brought on some laughter from two recruits who were waiting for them to get up. This was another mistake.

Willows went red in the face and confronted the two laughing recruits with a look that could kill at a hundred paces. "If you ever do that again, to a fellow member of your Platoon," he said "I will take your life. Is that clear?" "Yes" came the answer, apparently not loud enough. Willows bellowed "again!" "Yes Corporal Willows!" they replied.

The rest of the short march went on without incident. Tony and Keith were breathing quite heavily by the time they got to the hut. It was only eight in the morning, school was in and the teacher was already pissed.

"Get inside and stand by the beds you picked this morning" he said. "I will at that time, assign you a bed space that will be your home for the next eleven weeks. When you have your bed space, move your shit into it and stay there until I change things up."

Willows read the names and the bed spaces off to the Squad. The recruits moved to their assigned areas.

Tony looked around, breathed deeply and said "this is home." Willows ordered them to follow him around and proceeded to give them a tour of the hut, so they knew where things were.

They received a fire briefing including alarm stations and fire exits and a muster point in case they had to evacuate. He showed them where the smoking area was, the garbage huts and how to field strip a cigarette after use. Keith got near Tony during these tours and mumbled under his breath, "this is Stalag 17" and he moved away.

Willows told them they would be responsible to do fire pickets in the block every day and night and they should read and understand the Fire Orders that were posted in the front office. They then moved to the front office which was the information centre for their barrack area. He showed them the information boards where their course number was posted, along with their company, platoon number, section and squad.

Corporal Willows explained that members of this H Barrack formed "a platoon." Half of a platoon, or half the H Barrack was a section and one quarter of the H Barrack was a squad. There were 80 recruits in a platoon, and a squad consisted of 20 recruits. Each squad had their own assigned instructors. Tony's squad was blessed to be assigned to Corporals Willows and Miller.

They were course 7247, A Company, One Platoon and the squad's identification color was Red. All Willows said was "memorize it." Most of the classes would be done as a squad but most of the exercises would be done as a full platoon. Before and after classes and exercises the recruits would form up outside and march as a group to and from the barracks.

He also told them that their names would be posted alongside their weekly duties on these boards. They were expected to know what their assignments were at all times. Failure to complete a duty would be met with extra duties and counseling.

Some of these duties would include: Mailman, Newspaper Representative, Squad Senior, Course Senior, dining room rep, and points man while on the march. Each of these areas had a name next to it and they owned these duties for one week.

Sheet exchange was every Wednesday and a recruit was assigned to hand them out. This came along with the big one known as "cleaning stations." Everyone had a cleaning station that was changed every week. Everything from floors to showers to sinks to urinals was there and they all had names next to them. This was an area of great concern to all recruits. They scrambled to see what their first tasks were.

Keith got to the front of the pile fairly quickly and got out with great difficulty. Tony could see him smiling as he came up to him. "Well? What the hell, man, what are we doing?" Keith said "well Tony, I got sinks this week; all 14 of them." "Poor baby," Tony replied "what about me, Keith? What have they got me doing?" Keith smiled and put his head down and started to laugh. "Urinals, buddy, you're cleaning urinals." "Shit" Tony said. Keith laughed again and said "no Tony, that's next week" and he walked away.

Willows went on to explain what the duties for each station were and what was expected of them to pass inspection. Failure was not recommended.

Along with cleaning station duties, the recruits' personal hygiene was to be impeccable. Failure in this area would be met with a severe, negative chit written against them and training would follow.

Willows gave them the rules of the barracks that were to be followed at all times. These included: No hands in your pockets; No chewing gum; no leaning on walls; Recruits will come to attention when being approached by an NCO (Non-Commissioned Officer) and Personal problems were to be brought to the attention of the instructor immediately.

Tony and Keith were breathing deeply, thinking about how much work was ahead of them, and it was only noon. That meant time for lunch!

"You've got one minute to get outside and line up in ranks girls. From now on it will be three ranks when falling in. It's military talk, get used to it."

Down the road they went, like a broken machine, trying to hold it together with Willows chewing their asses at every opportunity, which was many.

Lunch was a disaster from start to finish. It was some kind of stew and western sandwiches were the mains along with what passed for soup and salad. Tony could feel his stomach tightening up, but he made it through. Thirty minutes later they were back in the barracks.

Bedding was issued from Stores and Willows said that the bed demonstration should be taken seriously and would be the one and only time he was going to show them.

As luck would have it, he picked Tony's bed area to do the demo and used Tony's sheets and blankets to show the recruits how to make a military bed. This was a bonus he thought. He was getting his bed made!

Everybody crowded around the bed space as Corporal Willows laid out the sheet on the mattress and folded it under, pulling it tight, very tight. He made a perfect 45 degree corner on the sheet at the head of the bed and folded it under, pulling it tight. All four corners were constructed the same way and were tight up against the mattress. The cover sheet was next on the bed, along with what he called a counter-pane and folded it ten inches down from the top of the bed because he had a ruler, making sure that the folded sheet was also ten inches. Cover sheet and counter-pane were folded flat over the foot of the mattress and again a 45 degree corner on the bed covering was completed. Bed covers were tucked under the mattress, front and back and pulled as tight as could be.

Next Willows took the grey fire blanket, folded it twice lengthways, placed it at the foot of the bed and tucked it under the mattress, tight. To complete the demo, he took the pillow and put it into a white cover and folded the ends under to make sure the pillow was 18 inches wide. This he centered at the head of the bed and made sure both sides, from the edge of the mattress, were the same. He did everything with his ruler. When he was done, it was a thing of beauty. It was clean, tight, flat and perfect. He took a quarter from his pocket and bounced it off the bed.

He then stood back and asked if there were any questions from his group. He answered them quickly and ordered them to their bed spaces to make their beds. As far as Tony could see, there was only one smart guy in the group. He asked Willows if he could borrow his ruler. This brought a smile to Willows' face.

The rest of the afternoon and evening was filled with recruits making and remaking their beds, until they had a good representation of Corporal Willows' demonstration.

Tony's bed did not escape being torn to pieces by the Instructor before he left the block, saying he'd be back at 1700 hours to take them to supper and their beds better be made. Tony could hear himself saying "what the hell is 1700 hours? More damn code."

No matter what, some guys just can't make beds. It took the help of many, and one ruler and many tries to get the task done. This was something that was going to take time and that was something they didn't have.

The back door opened suddenly and the cold air came in. It was Corporal Willows. The familiar bellow could be heard throughout the block. "You've got one minute to get your gear on and get outside. Form up in three ranks and stand still."

They hurried to get past him and get on the road. One minute came and past, then two, then three. Corporal Willows came out and called them to attention and marched them down to the Mess again.

Tony wasn't sure just how you could make a roast taste so bad, but he was sure that the beast didn't go down without a fight. It was tough as hell and he was convinced that he would not be putting on weight while he was there.

Thirty minutes later put them in front of the barracks, waiting to go inside. Thus ending day one from hell and getting some much needed sleep. Before Willows released them, he reminded them that all barrack duties were to begin this day and they had tasks that must be completed before inspection in the morning. After yelling "dismissed" Willows was gone.

Chapter 7

The tired recruits entered their barracks and were greeted by what could only have been a nuclear explosion in their sleeping area. The barracks had been torn apart, beds were everywhere and there wasn't a sheet on anything. Mattresses were even found in the laundry area.

Keith, who was next to Tony, was shaking his head in disbelief. How in the hell could that little shit do this in three minutes? Swearing and yelling could be heard in the barracks for the next hour or so as the recruits tried to make sense of the carnage and get their beds and areas back together.

Tony could see guys wandering by, mumbling to themselves about whether or not this was going to happen every day.

It was after 8:00 pm before the barracks was back together again and the recruits started looking closer at their block duties. Tony and Keith had help making their beds again by a few guys that had been in cadets before and knew how to make military beds. There were many tricks to making a proper military bed. Ironing the 45 degree corner flat was one of them. Ironing your pillow flat, so there were no wrinkles, was another. Crawling under the bed and pulling the sheets tight and hooking them around the springs was a secret.

Before the recruits moved on to help another, one of them looked into Tony's eyes and said quite seriously "the biggest thing you have to remember when making a military bed, is don't sleep in it."

Tony watched as guys were helping other guys get their beds made. He nodded to himself saying "this was a good thing."

Tony's bed space was about half way down the aisle and as he finished the bed mystery he looked at the guys around him. He hoped that they would become some of his best friends. Over time he would prove to be correct.

Keith was to his right, and he was sure there would be many a late night conversation over what was to come. To the right of Keith was a slender guy with glasses and a longer than average nose. He had a big voice and a smile for everyone. His name was Ron Van Meter.

To Tony's left was an intense dude named Rick Bagley. He had a wide-eyed stare and was always asking questions. To Rick's left was Ken Fanning. He was a nice guy that didn't ask a lot of questions at first. He just listened and shook his head a lot. Tony decided to nick-name him "Fanny." Fanny would prove to be a valued friend. To Fanny's left was what Tony deemed to be a "laid-back rocker." Nothing seemed to bother this guy. Steve Langley didn't get excited. He told Tony it was too early in the game to sweat the little stuff. Steve was a big guy, tall with a long pony-tail and a big mustache. He loved to listen to rock and roll on his head-set.

This unlikely group of people would probably have never met or hung out had they not each made the decision that landed them here. Yet here they were and would become the best of friends and would be known as "the rat pack."

Tony somehow knew that he was going to get along with these guys but true friends were hard to find. Tony started to think about Mark and a worried frown came over his face. Keith noticed this, but did not ask. It wasn't time.

Tony's mind slipped back to the good times that he and Mark had while sitting on Ma's stoop, talking about what they wanted to be when they grew up. Tony was growing up and moving on. He could see Mark, sitting alone on Ma's step.

The "pack" got together and read their station duties. These would have to be done every morning before inspection. Tony could see very early mornings and long days ahead of him. Tony scratched his head and said "how in the hell do you clean a urinal?" He hoped there would be gloves.

Tony counted 14 urinals in all and the mornings were the worst for usage. He found the materials he would need and went back to look at the monsters again. Porcelain, chrome and a smelly puck, how hard could it be? Tony forgot that other things ended up in the urinals also and every one of them would have to be scoured. Tomorrow would tell the tale and he would wait and watch which one of the urinals was used the most.

It was 10:00 pm and "lights out" was called. Things started to quiet down. Tony lay on top of his bed, trying hard not to mess it up. He put his pillow on the floor before he closed his eyes.

Sunday was to be the last "quiet" day before things started happening. They were to get accustomed to their surroundings and each other. Corporal Willows or a

Corporal Miller would take turns marching them to the Mess Hall for meals.

Everyone was looking forward to getting started. The day went by quickly and they all settled in at lights out. It took Tony awhile to fall asleep due to the apprehension and excitement of what was to come.

Chapter 8

It seemed only a second later Tony opened his eyes to what was the loudest noise he had ever heard. Garbage cans?

A garbage can flew past his bed and smashed into the wall. It made one hell of a noise. More cans were flying through the barracks and men were yelling and swearing as they hit the barrack lockers and the bed frames.

"Everyone up," someone yelled. "Get out of bed, you lazy bastards! School is in, and your teachers are not happy. What makes you think you can sleep your life away on the Queen's nickel? Get up!"

Tony saw a bed being turned upside down with a recruit still in it, a guy named Watson. Corporal Willows was not alone! He had a partner that they had not seen before. His name was Corporal Miller and he was hell on wheels and just as noisy as Willows. "My name is Miller, Corporal

Miller to you pussers and if I hear different, you won't see the sun until spring. I'm here to mold you miserable civilians into military men, or die trying. If you think you can't measure up or you made a big mistake in being here; now's the time to hit the tracks!"

You could hear Miller's voice throughout the barracks. He was only average height and build but his voice and mannerisms were eight feet high and you could feel yourself turning to salt under his gaze. "Twice the horror," Tony thought.

Most of the guys in the sleeping area were up and getting their clothes on as the devil's children walked quickly by destroying anything that was within their reach. Some of the guys weren't so lucky and the two instructors descended on them like hungry dogs looking for a weak spot.

"You pussy's have 30 minutes to shit, shower, shave, and form up outside. That means making your rack up too girls," Miller said. "We will be taking a quick look at that mess too. That's a warning Marys, now move!"

The place exploded into movement as the two instructors went into the front office to wait the time out.

Tony finally had a second to look at his watch. It was 5:10 in the god-damn morning! Beds made, he hoped, shit, shower, shave and out the door into the cold Nova Scotia morning they rushed just as Willows and Miller burst open the door and lit the air up with threats of hell itself if they didn't start to shape up now.

Willows said "this morning is your first lessons sweethearts, so heed them well."

They called the men to attention and spent the next minute going up and down the ranks eating everybody's face and threatening to put pace sticks up their ass if they didn't straighten up. This got the recruits' attention fast. Corporal Willows ended his tirade when he stopped in front of Recruit Watson. "What's the matter Watson? Why are you sweating like a pig? What's wrong with your eyes, boy? Look at me. Are you in pain? Why are you twitching?" Recognition fell on Willows' face. His voice went calm. "Step out of line Watson and stand by the barracks' door."

Corporal Willows approached Corporal Miller and they spoke quietly for a minute or two and then Corporal Miller walked over to Recruit Watson and led him back into the barracks.

Willows brought the next command in. "Left turn!" he yelled. Berating came in bunches. After many a left turn, the guys finally got it together and they moved out. Willows called out "Quick march!" and he started yelling "left, right, left, right!" He was screaming at them to "listen to the cadence! When we call left, your left foot should be on the ground."

It was a long march to the Mess, and even longer as Willows hovered over them at breakfast and urged them to move along. "Save some of that food for the rest of the men Recruit Welding! It already looks to me that you ate all the pies your mamma baked you!"

Tony didn't remember breakfast, only the chewing Willows gave him on the way back to the barracks for being out of step. It was going to be a long, long day.

Back in the barracks Willows and Miller took them around to every one of their cleaning stations and ripped them all new assholes. Nothing was to the standard that they needed to be, in order for the recruits to get a passing grade. What they would get was a "shitty chitty" which was a written warning that things needed to pick up quickly.

They found dust and grime on everything they touched. They even checked inside the shower drain for Christ's sake, Tony noted. He also noted that there were strange things floating in his urinals that weren't there earlier on.

The floors needed to shine from one end to the other. Miller showed them how to use the polisher and every bed space was to look like brand new.

The guys had a long way to go and it was only day two.

The instructors warned them that they had better start pulling together or people would be going home. There was no break, "get your shit on and form up outside in three ranks and don't forget the paperwork you brought with you or you won't be getting paid."

There was more marching, more terrorizing, "left, right, left, right. You've got less than a hundred days and nights to get this right, just you and me."

Tony was sure Willows was a mad-man.

07:30 AM found the recruits in a building numbered 140 and in a classroom numbered B10 with their Leave Passes and Birth Certificates. They'd be filling in more paperwork and then they would be issued combat clothing, gym clothing, and Canadian Forces dress uniforms and work clothing. They were all given appointments by the public health nurse for eye tests, x-rays, and dental if needed. Pay documents were filled out and given to the Duty Sergeant.

They were all shown where the MIR (Medical Inspection Room) was located.

When all the paperwork was completed, they headed for the CANEX (Canadian Exchange Store) to buy personal items like boot polish, cleaning rags, toothpaste and of course a ruler. This building also housed the well-known Base Barbershop which they had to visit once a week.

They had all heard the horror stories about the Base barbers and how they had an evil sense of humour when it came to new recruits. It was already late in the morning by the time One Platoon got to the shop and they lined up in the CANEX Foyer to take their turns.

Chapter 9

All you can say was fast and furious was the game. There was a rumour going around that everyone should try to stay away from the barber with the glasses. Problem with that was when they walked in the room they noticed that all four barbers were wearing glasses.

The guys moved in four at a time and 30 seconds later they came out like sheared sheep or worse. They came out rubbing their heads where their hair had been. They all had that deer in the headlight look.

The recruits were going through at quite a pace when all of a sudden the buzzers stopped and there was silence. Tony and Keith looked in the door and their eyes opened wide with amazement. It was coffee break and the barbers were heading for the food court, leaving the guys seated in mid-haircut. They either had half a cut, one side only, down the middle only or Mohawks. A poor shit named Parsons had been fully shaved on one side of his head. Everyone looked in and broke out laughing until Corporal Miller came up to the offenders and threatened to rip their heads off. Everything went quiet.

The barbers returned and silently dared the recruit sitting in the chair to make a comment. Tony and Keith were next in the weed whacker chairs and felt the cool, Nova Scotia air on their domes the moment the hair was gone. They looked like everybody else coming out of that room. Bald eggs with glasses, it was official, they were in Boot Camp!

A two ton shuttle bus was put on for the recruits to move from the CANEX to their next appointments around the Base, including lunch. This was a welcome relief from marching but talking was still not permitted.

They moved to the supply stores, it was time to get "kitted up." There was just too much clothing to carry around at one time and the warmth of the bus kept their heads warm.

Clothing stores was a machine in motion. Everything was practiced before and perfected down to the shoe-laces. The recruits were lined up in two rows; one for daily work dress and parade dress; known as CF Greens, complete. This included shoes, boots, hats, rubbers and gloves. They were given a barrack box which they put their clothing into and deposited them in the shuttle in their seating area.

The other row was "combat issue." Everything down to boots and helmets was issued. Cold weather kit was also issued including muck-lucks and warm socks. A duffle bag was also issued and the combat gear was placed in the bag and put on the bus.

The last thing the recruits were given going out the door was their cap badge. It was a military crest known as "the cornflake." It was a proud moment for all on the bus on their way back to the barracks.

Back in the barracks, the instructors advised the course that the shuttle was also laid on for the next day to take them to the MIR for their infamous needle called the "pusser shot." It was like being hit in the arm with a baseball bat, it stung so much.

Eye glasses would be checked and combat spectacles would be issued. Recruits with dental requirements would be set up for a later appointment. These appointments were expected to take most of the day.

That night the recruits were expected to stencil their names on all their clothing using a black tube marker with a roller ball on the end. Their names would be located on the tails of their shirts, bottom of shorts and on gym gear. This task took most of the evening and for some into the night. There were just so many markers and some kept clogging.

Tony and the pack got together as a team and got their marking done in just a few hours. While they sat marking their kit the discussion turned to Recruit Watson and the fact that they had noticed his bed space was empty. One of the pack members heard that Watson had been going through Cocaine withdrawal and had been removed from the course, pending military discipline. It was clear to the pack that they wouldn't be doing any messing around.

As Tony looked at his kit he imagined himself wearing his combats and running through the woods. Before the instructors left the block, they told the recruits to just put the clothing in their lockers and the next day they would be given instruction on how to iron every piece and put them in the lockers correctly. Also, they would be packing away their civilian clothing and only wearing coveralls and sneakers in the barracks from then on. The sneakers were worn because the floor had to be spotless at all times.

The instructors were gone in a heartbeat and the recruits were left to finish their barrack duties and pack away their new clothes. Some of the guys were learning how to use the floor polisher, which is not as easy as Miller had shown them. It kept going in different directions and was slamming into lockers and walls.

Tony's cleaning station, the urinals, would wait until the morning because he had a plan to make his life easier.

5:00 AM comes early in recruit school. Tony was already awake and under his bed tightening the sheets to make sure there were no wrinkles. The measurements were then checked with his new ruler.

Some of the recruits took to ironing the corners of their sheets just to lay them flat. Tony couldn't bounce a quarter off his bed, but it was close. He ran to his cleaning station and started to watch the urinals to see what the traffic was like. He had come up with a plan to shut down most of the pissers in the morning so as to have only a few to contend with before inspection; and it worked!

This day would be the last day they'd be in civilian clothes. From now on it was the military way, all the way. At 5:30 AM Willows stuck his head in and bellowed that the Squad had two minutes to form up outside. Willows told the Squad he didn't go into the barracks because he didn't want to see the shit hole until they started cleaning it properly and that was going to start that day.

Bald heads and civilian clothes was the name of the game today. The food was still bad and the other recruits still looked at them and snickered. Tony knew this was going to change. The only thing that did not change was the miserable instructors constantly yelling in their faces "move it, move it, move it!" "Listen to what you recruits are doing to this cadence! Mary mother and Joseph there's not one brain in the whole lot of you," Corporal Miller screamed from the rear of the gaggle.

Back in the block at 6:30 AM, Tony and Keith ran to their bed spaces only to find that the barracks had been trashed again. "Not up to standards, ladies; not up to standards!" was all they heard. It was a mystery. How in the hell did those evil bastards trash the bed spaces again when they were with us all the time?

Keith was mumbling and shaking his head.

Chapter 10

Miller got the Squad together in the TV room and told them that they were going to split in half with one group going on medical duties and the other would be instructed on how to iron uniforms and set up lockers. When the tasks were completed, they would switch locations and complete the day.

Corporal Willows would be staying behind to give the demonstrations and Corporal Miller took the rest of the recruits to the MIR to finish their in-routine.

The roll call was made to separate the groups and the day began in a flurry.

Corporal Miller left with his group as soon as the bus arrived.

Corporal Willows ordered ironing boards set up in the laundry area. Everyone stood wide-eyed around the instructor as his lesson began in earnest. He went through the proper way to iron a shirt, pants, underwear, towels and shorts. He showed them where the creases were to be and how to avoid a double-crease.

The guys had never seen socks ironed before, let alone rolled up in such a way as to make them look like hotdogs. Corporal Willows was serious about it too. Tony was shaking his head again. "Something about this you don't understand Simons?" Willows growled. "No Corporal," Tony responded, like it was automatic or something.

Corporal Willows was no fool when it came to giving his lecture. With his demonstration completed, the recruits asked questions about certain procedures. He said in a loud voice "everyone will complete this task by tomorrow morning and be in proper work dress, ready to start the day." He ordered them to study the pictures they had in the office as to what proper work dress looked like and be standing by their beds at 0800 hours for inspection.

Willows smiled again and said "what's the matter ladies is there something missing?" A "yes, Corporal Willows" came the response from the back of the group. "How does all this kit go into the locker?" was the question. "Follow me ladies, old Corporal Willows wouldn't leave you hanging in the wind."

He moved to the first locker in the row of bed spaces that was still empty, but the locker had a lock on it. He spun it a few times and opened the door to reveal a fully-equipped locker complete with everything ironed, measured and the creases were as sharp as a knives.

No detail was missed. The gym shorts were 9 by 9 inches; the towels were 9 by 9; underwear was 4 by 4; work shirts were 9 by 12; the CF Scarf was 7 by 7 and the sweater was 9 by 12. Everything had a specific measurement and placement. The rest were hung on the rod, hooks in.

Corporal Willows stepped back and looked at his charges. "Just like this, ladies, now get to it."

The other half of the Squad came back protecting their arms where they had received "the pusser shot." They were shown the same demo, along with the same completed locker while Tony's group was off to get their shots. When they returned the barracks turned into a hive of activity. Course 7247 was coming alive!

Chapter 11

The recruits were given more and more to do over the rest of the week. All of this was to test their limits of stress and endurance. The instructors' constant growling, kit inspections and stand by your bed inspections were done every morning. Of course there were the "surprise inspections."

Not being able to leave the barracks was already wearing on some of the recruits and it was beginning to show. Tony could hear them in the night, moving around in the dark, trying to get their stations ready for morning inspection, only to be ripped apart again by Willows and Miller.

Tony and the rat pack made sure their shit was done and inspected by the guys before lights out. They felt it was the only way. They all agreed they'd have to work together.

There's no place to hide when there's 80 guys around you, all trying to do the same thing. Shining boots and shoes was new for most of the guys and became a major problem. They had to shine like glass each morning or they'd sale across the barracks, smashing into the wall.

Tony could hear "more work on your boots Evans!" as it went flying past Tony's face. They hated to wear them, but they had to. It was all part of them trying to tear the guys down in order to build them up again. Tony thought it was like they were driving the civilian elements out of them and replacing them with military elements.

The marching was constant and the complaining was too; but the guys knew they were somehow getting better because they understood what was being asked of them.

It was after morning inspection on the Monday of the first week of actual classes when Corporal Willows told the Squad that the schedule that day would start with "PT" (physical training) and it would be that way, everyday from then on. Tony remembered seeing it coming up on the schedule and wondered what it would be like.

Corporal Miller made an appearance but was not alone. He had a recruit with him. He was directed to the bed space previously occupied by Watson.

The Squad learned that the new recruit, whose name was Jim Bennet had been "recoursed" because of illness.

Down to the gym they marched and into a huge recreational facility to line up in the Hall. They were introduced to a no-neck PERI (Physical Education Requirements Instructor) named "Dane." His lot in life was to make them into men. That's what he said anyway.

"Into your gym kit ladies and move onto the floor. This is where we make you pay for all that pie you ate or the buns you ate that your mamma gave you."

Running, jumping, dodge ball, pushups, sit-ups and the rope climb were on the menu from now on. In order to pass PT they would be required to do 30 sit-ups, 30 pushups, and a mile and a half run in under 12 minutes. Let's not forget drown proofing.

Tony and Keith had never run in their lives, let alone timed it. The instructor put them on the floor and they tried pushups and sit-ups. That was a mistake, the guys looked real bad.

The instructor told them that they had better start practicing in the hut after hours. They were to try a mile and a half run in the gym while being timed. Tony ended up puking, and Van Meter pulled a hamstring. The instructor was disgusted and vowed to get them into shape. PT every morning was designed to shape them up and it did. They got stronger and could run farther than they ever could before.

The most challenging exercise came later, drown proofing. They were to be put into very large coveralls and jump off a very high tower into the pool. They were then supposed to float there for 10 minutes without moving a muscle.

Tony and Keith had no problem with this move. They both lived next to a lake and swam most of their lives. Others in the pack were not so lucky. Bagley couldn't swim a stroke and went down to the bottom like a rock. Two guys had to rescue him and another extended a pole he could grab onto to drag him to the side of the pool.

This did not deter the instructor. For many days after that, Bagley would be going off the tower until eventually he figured it out.

Fanning kept lifting his head up to breath and the instructor would ball him out. The guys didn't know it yet, but PT would be the best thing they ever experienced. Over time they came to enjoy the gym. Everyone was looking forward to the tests.

Classroom training started after PT and continued in the afternoon before drill. A myriad of subjects: General Service knowledge; Command Structure; Rank Identification; Military Law; and First Aid were on the schedule in the next weeks. The recruits would be tested on this knowledge, pass or fail.

Tony thought to himself "more stress." He and the rat pack would quiz each other in the barracks at night as they polished their shoes and boots and worked on sit-ups and pushups.

Chapter 12

More recruits were losing it. They would report to "sick call" in the mornings before gym complaining of stomach problems or "pulled somethings." These were the recruits that were not going to make it. One morning, they were just gone. Others would ask to be released for all kinds of reasons; medical, family and anything else they could come up with. This, however, was not happening. They had signed the line and would have to do at least six months in uniform before they could again ask to be released. These guys disappeared also but rumour had it that they had gone down the tracks, AWOL (Absent Without Leave).

Tony's Platoon had a couple of strange guys show their true selves during the early weeks and were taken away. A recruit named Blackmore was hard to wake up in the morning and the instructors even dumped him out of his bed. He slept until he woke up on his own. The medics finally took him out on a stretcher, still sleeping. He was gone too.

Recruit Welding mixed up a strange concoction of cleaning fluids and wax stripper, and god knows what else to strip his floor quicker around his bed space. He ended up gassing the entire block and everyone had to be evacuated until the Fire Department cleared the building; it was amazing.

The most dangerous man they had in the barracks was Brazzer. How this guy passed the psyche test was a mystery to Tony and the pack, yet here he was. He never really fit in. He was always on the outside of things, quiet and unassuming. He could never figure out how to wear his uniform properly, and his shoes were the worst in the Platoon. He always looked like he was wearing a bag and he really didn't want to be there. He kept saying that he wanted to go home and complained to anyone that would listen. His cleaning station was the shower room floor and all he had to do was wipe it down with disinfectant and a mop. This was not Brazzer's style. Somehow he got it in his head to wipe the floor down with his heavy grey socks on, because he had them on anyway. Then he'd roll them back up and put them back in his shitty locker.

Corporals Willows and Miller reported to Sergeant Akern and from time to time the Sergeant would inspect their barracks. During morning inspection of Brazzer's locker, Sergeant Akern was ripping him a new asshole, because it was such a pit. He grabbed one of Brazzer's grey socks from the locker and was about to tell him to roll it tighter when a horrible scream came from his mouth "you idle little crow! You're fucking with me, aren't you, Recruit?" came out of his mouth. The Sergeant had grabbed the sock and squeezed it. Water or some kind of liquid came out of the sock, streamed down his arm into his uniform and onto the floor.

They were already confined to barracks so Brazzer was given even more extra duties and the Sergeant stomped away saying he needed a drink.

Brazzer was finally taken away in handcuffs when he threatened to set fire to the barracks in the night and kill us all.

Being confined to barracks does strange things to people. Their true personalities come out because there is no place to hide. Guys were still being found with drugs or they were found with alcohol on their breath and were arrested. Where they got the booze and drugs was a mystery.

The sick, lame and lazy were discovered, and dealt with quickly. Tony and Keith really doubted if there would be anyone left to graduate. The last big menace that showed himself was a guy named Buckles. He was found roaming the barrack floors at night, carrying a bayonet and bending over guys while they slept. Where he got the knife no one knew. Two recruits woke up and grabbed him in the hallway, took the knife away from him and held him down until the MP's came and hauled him away.

The recruits that were ousted were again replaced by recourse recruits who were in a course ahead but had fallen behind for some reason and were being given another shot.

Chapter 13

Every day was just about the same, they were up at
0500 hours (the 2400 hour clock they were now used to);
then marched to the Mess Hall. They marched on their own
now. Then there were workstations and morning inspections
that seemed to be getting better.

PT was a good way to start the day and Tony was
feeling pretty good about himself in that area. The afternoon
found them in classrooms, learning all things military and
they were being tested on First Aid which they were told
they would use in upcoming field exercises.

One of the biggest problems the guys were having was
drill. Getting 20 guys to move together was one thing but
getting them to march together was a "royal cluster fuck," as
Corporal Miller would say. The Drill Hall was long and
open, so you could hear the slightest noise on the floor. If
you weren't moving together you knew it, and worst yet, the
instructors knew it. They drilled every day, up and down the

Hall, learning the different movements while being chewed on by the instructors.

It was never good enough. "Don't you eyeball me, you little shit," they could hear from the instructors from the other side of the Hall. "Your other left Fanning, you little puke!" The instructors were relentless, but the Squad was getting it.

Starting on the second Friday afternoon the Platoon was involved in the graduation parade. This meant that the Platoon graduating would take the lead position on the parade square and each course would fall behind them ending with the newest course.

This gave Tony and the guys a look at what they were working toward and they could see their positions move closer to the front as the weeks progressed.

Chapter 14

Tony was always watching the training schedule further along and he saw things that were concerning to him, things like "Heartbreak Hill, the Gas Hut, and the 10-Mile Run." "Jesus Christ," was all he could say to himself.

As he moved away from the schedule, he smiled to himself, "Weapons in week five, and maybe a beer!"

It was getting close to Christmas and Tony, Keith and the guys were advised that they would be going home for eight days and they all thought that it would be great!

Tony was lying in his bed the night before they were to leave. It was quiet, except for the occasional snoring. He thought about how he had been missing Betty and wondered how she was doing. He thought about how he would feel, being back in Port Nichols. He would finally find out how Mark was. He wondered how the guys in the barracks would feel about him if they found out about his past. A lot of things had changed; he had changed.

The recruits were told that they would be in S3's; full military formal dress; and were to conduct themselves as members of the Canadian Forces at all times. Little did they know that the worst possible thing they could do was to take a break in the middle of training. It would mean they would be pushed even harder when they got back. That was the last thing on Tony's mind right now.

Leave Passes were issued, Travel Orders were cut for the recruits and the travel day finally arrived. The guys would be bused to Halifax, a military plane to Trenton and everyone including the rat pack would be scattered to the winds from there.

Tony and Ron Van Meter were heading for Port Nichols. Keith and the rest of the pack were headed west. They all agreed to meet up in Trenton on their return. Tony knew the trip would take all day and a change was already happening to his and Ron's Travel Orders. They would fly to Toronto and Bus to Port Nichols.

The flight to Trenton was great and Tony and Ron got to know each other better. It seemed that Ron only lived a few miles from Port Nichols. They flew into Toronto in the middle of the night, during a snow storm. With the storm raging, most buses were not running. Tony and Ron had to hang around the terminal until 0700 hours. That was when the next buses were scheduled to go.

Being in the Toronto Bus Terminal in the middle of the night isn't great at the best of times but the storm and the cold brought all the street people in to warm up and get out of the weather.

Everything was closed inside the terminal except for an old newspaper stand that was run by a nasty-looking old lady that wanted to know what the hell these two pigeons were doing here at this time of the morning.

Tony managed a "waiting for a bus, ma'am." She looked at them and cackled "you're not going to make it sonny, unless you and your buddy get in here behind me and stay put," she said. She came closer to Tony and said "look around."

Tony and Ron looked up and saw that the street wolves were moving in for the kill. Shady street characters were moving in closer, begging for money and asking them if they were in the military. A couple of dried up old hookers were moving in, offering them a good time for little money.

Ron's eyes widened and the old newspaper lady saw his fear. "Get in here and stay behind me," she said. "These street buzzards won't touch you in here. The terminal opens at 6 o'clock and then more people will be here. You're safe for now," she said and turned back to continue what she was doing.

The guys had new respect for this street tough old woman.

0600 hours rolled around, the terminal opened up and the old lady kicked them out and told them to have more common sense next time.

They moved toward the loading area, not looking back, or they would have seen the old newspaper lady shake her head and smile.

The guys were in Port Nichols within the hour and Ron's parents where there to pick him up. Ron introduced Tony to them. They asked Tony what he was doing for Christmas and told him that they'd be very happy to have him spend the holidays with them if he wanted.

Tony thanked them and said he had "people" he wanted to visit and he told Ron he'd see him back at the terminal in seven days. Tony walked into the terminal and called a cab. He gave the driver the address to Liz's rooming house. He sat back in the cab and looked around. It had been about five weeks but it seemed like forever.

The cab stopped in front of the rooming house and Tony stepped out to be greeted by a huge hug from Liz with a tear in her eye. She stepped back and looked proudly at the military man in front of her. "My god," she said "look what you've become."

"I need a room for a few days," Tony said "can you help?" She hugged him again and hurried him into the house. "You stay as long as you want, this is your home." She got him a big cup of coffee and they sat at the table, talking for a long time. "Have you slept at all Tony?" she asked. "You look tired." Tony told her about Toronto and the newspaper lady and that he had indeed been up all night.

Chapter 15

Liz took him to the same room he had stayed in before and told him to rest. He didn't remember taking off his uniform or getting into the bed and closing his eyes. What seemed like moments later, he was startled awake by a banging on his door and a big booming voice "get up boy, open the door!" Mo yelled.

Tony cracked the door a bit and found himself looking Mo right in the eye. He opened the door wide and Mo grabbed him in a bear-hug so tightly he thought a rib cracked. "Welcome home, Tony, you've been missed! How long can you stay?"

Tony explained that he had to be heading back in about a week. He wanted to visit with Liz and Mo over the holidays and try to see Olive and Mark while he was there.

They sat in the kitchen for the rest of the afternoon and into the evening talking about what Tony was going through at the recruit school. Tony asked Mo if he had heard what happened in the war with the Lords. Tony had been planning to ask Mark about what happened but if Mo had heard talk at the bar, he was all ears.

Mo told Tony that, talk at the Franklin was that the Army met up with the Lords just North of Toronto on an abandoned airstrip and all hell had broken loose. Guns, chains, knives and even bikes themselves were used to try to destroy each other. Some of the guys that got there late said they had never seen so many angry men with one thing on their minds, that was to destroy each other or die trying.

Mo didn't have all the information, only that by the time the police got there, it was mostly over and each side was dragging away dead and injured.

Tony looked at Mo and could only say "Jesus Christ."

It was late in the evening, but Tony called Olive and told her he was in town and that they'd get together in the next day or so. He also asked if Mark was ok. Olive was happy to hear from him and couldn't wait to see him. She told Tony that Mark was fine and she would get in touch with him and let him know that he was in town.

The next morning was Christmas Eve day and Tony was in the kitchen with Liz and Mo having coffee and toast. It was good to be back together again. Tony felt like he had been away a long time. He was going to visit Olive today and say hello to the kids that were still living with her. He told Liz not to wait up and that he would take a cab back later. More coffee and conversation and then Tony was out the door, heading first for the pier and then to Olive's.

Tony walked along the pier, remembering how he felt just before he left. This time he was looking into some of the little shops that were still open so that he could purchase a few small gifts for Liz, Olive and the girls. An hour later he hailed a cab with his purchases. He found some perfume, hair combs and candles that he knew all girls seemed to like and thought this would do the trick.

As the cab rolled up to the townhouse, Tony could see the old Chevy van parked outside so he knew that Mark was inside, waiting. Tony came through the door, hugged Olive and whispered in her ear "I'm back, Ma I missed you." She hugged him back and said "welcome home." The girls all gave him a hug and then were off to do what girls do.

Tony looked over to see his friend Mark coming towards him. He gave him a hug, and lifted him off his feet. Tony noticed the cast was gone. "Jesus, it's good to see you man, I couldn't believe it when Ma phoned and said you were here! You look good Tony, and you've put on some muscle."

The two friends sat and talked most of the day. Tony talked about the military and what he was going through and Mark talked about the club and the fight outside of Toronto.

Mark said that he had arrived there late because of traffic, so there wasn't much left to do, other than drive over a few of the Lords' bikes as they tried to get away. It had been a major shit-show and more people died that day. Many were arrested. Kevin and his commanders and the Lords' leader were in jail facing lengthy prison sentences for their part in the battle. Skip was elected Interim President of the Army until further notice. "Holy shit," was all Tony could say.

Mark said that his arm was still in a lot of pain at times, but Skip had been giving him some pills that really helped and made him feel good.

The rest of the day was a blur but good times were had by all. Olive told Tony to spend the night and have Christmas dinner with them the next day.

Christmas morning came and Tony retrieved the gifts he had brought. The girls were tickled and went screaming to their rooms with their new found booty. Olive was beside herself with the act of kindness. Even Mark was taken aback by the gift Tony had brought him from Cornwallis, a military lighter he had bought at the CANEX.

Christmas dinner was awesome and Tony and Mark restated their life-long friendship as Tony's cab pulled up to the house. Olive cried and Mark slapped his back, telling him to be careful and to call if he needed anything.

Tony knew that he wasn't going to be back for a long while, but didn't tell them. He said goodbye and climbed into the cab.

Back at Liz's, Tony told her how the visit went and how sad he would be to leave. He had to get back soon and finish what he had started. Before Tony went to bed Christmas Day he gave out the last of his gifts to Liz and Mo. They too were over the moon with the thoughtfulness of this young man. Liz then gave Tony a beautiful scarf that she had knitted. Tony went to his room and fell asleep with a full heart.

The rest of the time in Port Nichols went quickly and before he knew it, Mo was driving him to the Bus Terminal and shaking his hand. "Be safe" he said, and then he was gone.

Chapter 16

Tony found Ron in the coffee shop and they talked about their holidays until it was time to board and head for Trenton. Bus rides being what they are, you just sleep most of the way. Before they knew it, they were in Trenton AMU. This time; however, they were in uniform.

The flight to Halifax was the same as the first time, exciting! The bus to Cornwallis was also the same only this time it was too damn quick. They were back with a day to spare. It was Sunday and training would begin again on Monday.

Tony used the time to get his head back in the game and set up for a very busy week. All his buddies were showing up throughout the day and getting together to talk about the break and being home. All agreed that it was a great break but they would shortly find out that they would pay dearly for the holiday.

Keith eventually came through the door and Tony slapped him on the back and poked at him. "Heard you weren't coming back, K.G.; something about a bar fight in Saskatoon over some native lady with questionable virtues." Keith broke out laughing and said that he had given her Tony's number and said that she should call him.

They all agreed that it was good to be back and they started to check their kit for the next day. They wandered off to the office to find out what the week's duties would be.

Everybody had to do floors, it was a no-brainer, but this week Tony was assigned the smoker and the TV room. Keith had the laundry room, including the washers and dryers. This week would be different. This was the last week for wearing work dress. They would be into combats and weapons would be drawn. It was going to be amazing!

The Platoon stayed in uniform to march down to the Mess Hall. It was nice to look like everybody else. The rat pack was sitting near the door and in came a bunch of brand new recruits. They were still in civilian clothing, and long hair. An instructor was going up and down the line, growling at them repeatedly for talking and looking around.

Tony looked at Keith and said "did we look like that, man? No wonder everyone was staring at us." The guys' eyes went up and down the line of "fresh meat," trying to decide who would not make it and who would be another guy like Buckles.

Back in the barracks found the rat pack checking each other to make sure their kit was up to passing an inspection.

Chapter 17

Week five started out like being in a nuclear explosion. 0500 hours found the barrack lights on and garbage cans were flying down the aisles like paper in a windstorm. Corporals Willows and Miller had entered the barracks early to greet the recruits back to hell. In doing so, they caught most of the little darlings sleeping on top of their blankets. This was met with more garbage can lids being smashed into the lockers as startled recruits were being hauled from their beds. Mattresses and lockers were relocated to other parts of the building.

"Stand by your beds you miserable herd," Miller screamed! The next half hour was right out of a horror story. The instructors annihilated the recruits for being away and said that they would have to be trained all over again. They yelled and howled at them for not sleeping in their beds and because they had tried to pull a fast one on the old Corporals that were just there to help and guide them.

"You're going to pay for this!" Willows screamed.

Two more Corporals showed up out of nowhere with clipboards and started calling out the recruits' names. They told them to stand by their cleaning stations. Now there were four hounds from hell and they moved around the barracks and common areas ripping the recruits from top to bottom for not having their stations ready for inspection at any time of the day or night.

The recruits heard the words "shit pit" several dozen times. A new threat entered the instructors' vocabulary and the guys were not ready for Corporal Miller using it. "Bloody awful," he screamed. "Drop and give me twenty!"

These bastards were everywhere including the TV room and Smoker, to Tony's dismay.

"Recruit Simons," Willows howled! "Yes Corporal Willows" was his fast reply. "Do you have a valid driver's license?" Tony blinked, "yes Corporal," he said. "Well then find a broom and drive it over here. This floor is a shit show!" Willows continued his attack "what is your secondary duty?" he asked. "The Smoker," Tony replied. Willows looked at him and said "let's see if you can cock that up too, Simons."

Out the door they went into the dark and snowy morning. It wasn't hard to see that this was not going to be

Tony's day and it hadn't even gotten started. There were butts everywhere and some of the white painted rocks that formed a circle were turned over or were out of place. Tony melted under Willows' gaze. "Besides writing you up, Simons, I'm going to give you an extra duty. Go over to the garbage hut and find the nastiest can."

Tony bolted to the garbage hut and returned with a smelly, nasty can. Before Willows turned to walk back to the barracks he hissed "tomorrow morning, Recruit, my office and it better shine like glass! That can stays with you in your bed space until I release it back to the garbage hut tomorrow. Do you understand what I am telling you?" "Yes Corporal," Tony replied.

Willows entered the barracks and reminded the shell-shocked troops that inspection was still at 0800 hours, so they had better get their ass in gear. As Willows left the building, he yelled "welcome back ladies!"

"Holy Shit," was all anyone could say. There would be no breakfast today. The barracks was a whirl-wind of motion and not much talking. The guys knew what needed to be done and they only had three hours to do it.

Beds were moved back to their spaces and made; lockers were repositioned and their contents put back on the shelves. Tony polished his bed space and positioned the can in the middle of the area. He ran to the TV room and straightened everything he could find, putting a chair in front of the door to keep people out.

The Smoker was another thing. Rocks had to be repositioned and any butts he found had to be field-stripped and put in the smoker can. Everybody was helping everybody. It was the only way to get it all done and they knew it. Inspection had to go well. There was no other option.

Chapter 18

The instructors came back to a well-organized barracks with recruits in work dress, standing by their beds. Tony's garbage can looked out of place but the instructors didn't seem to notice it. Everything was checked and only minor slip-ups were noted. Tony could see that they were looking and wanted to find something though.

Willows reminded them that today's lesson would be on the gas mask, so leaving it behind would be a bad idea. Tony had checked the schedule and the mask was already hanging from his belt around his waist.

A quick march down to the gym found the PERI Instructor, Corporal Dane waiting for the group in the middle of the gym floor. "So you're back! Let's see how much turkey you ate," he said. "I bet you little shit-birds didn't do one pushup all the time you were away! Now let's see if I'm right! Get on the floor ladies and give me twenty pushups. When that's done, I'll take twenty sit-ups."

Corporal Dane was possessed. He ran the group hard the whole time they were there. It was awful and the Squad knew they were going to pay dearly for their time away.

Marching out in the cold to their next class, Tony kept smiling and caught Keith's eye and whispered "what the hell are you grinning about man, that was brutal?" Tony whispered back "we get to have a beer Friday, K.G.!" Keith smiled "beer!"

The March over to B140 took about 15 minutes and classroom B10, they already knew by heart. Sitting at their desks with the gas masks in front of them, Corporal Willows and Corporal Miller went over the characteristics of the mask and why it was so important to carry it with them when they were in unfamiliar terrain or known enemy territory.

They were shown how to take it from the carrier with their eyes closed, put it on and do seal checks before yelling "gas, gas, gas." This was to alert their troop or platoon of chemical danger. Every time they heard those words, they would put their mask on. They practiced the rest of the morning. By the time the class was over, they could get their masks on correctly in "under nine seconds." This was mandatory.

Along with the mask drill they learned how to get into their chemical suits and button up with gas masks on. The instructor warned them that they must be ready to react to a gas alert at any time. The mask and chemical suits were then removed and put back in their bags. Class over, the recruits were marched over to the Mess Hall.

To Tony's surprise, the food actually tasted pretty good. Lunch was quick and the guys were marched back to their barracks, got out of their work dress for the last time and put on combat dress for the first time in their lives. They checked each other over to see that all were dressed properly and that no strings were hanging out.

It was then time for drill. The guys knew that they were going to be torn to hell by the instructors. Rumour had it that there was going to be a Platoon Sergeant there to check on their progress. The recruits looked like actual military men in their combats. The guys were really proud to wear them.

Inside the Drill Hall, Sergeant Akern was already there and watched them enter. He moved to the Corporals to get a briefing. Then he stood back and watched Corporal Willows call the recruits to attention. He moved the recruits around the Hall and called the cadence as they moved. It didn't take long for the shit to hit the fan. Guys were not listening to simple commands that they had heard and tried many times before.

Bringing them to a halt had them crashing into each other like it was their first day. Everything they were not supposed to do, they were doing. It was like they were learning to walk again. The Sergeant was starting to lose it from his vantage point and the recruits could hear him yelling. "Stop that cow-kicking you miserable herd." This was his way of telling you that your left foot was coming down behind you instead of in front of you.

He was getting red in the face and started to pace. "Drive that foot down hard when you stop! If you break it, we'll get you another one."

The Corporals were taking the recruits through drill movements but things were getting steadily worse instead of better. The recruits were nervous and mistakes were coming in bunches. They had been at it for nearly three hours and you could tell that they had peaked the hour before. They were not going to get any better today. The Sergeant had to stick it to them one more time before he left.

He moved to the centre of the Drill Hall and waited for them to march by. "Now listen up you herd. I watched the instructors take you through your drill movements and girls, I'm not impressed. I don't smoke, I don't drink and I'm pretty tired of chasing my wife around the bedroom, so I can stay here all night long, if that's what you want."

You could hear a pin drop in the Hall when the instructors called "halt." Willows moved over to the Sergeant and spoke to him in a low voice. The Sergeant's head went up and he backed up a step and a look of disbelief came over his face. "No God Damn way!" he said. "It's that time already?" he barked out. "I wouldn't issue these animals a bag of rocks to defend themselves, let alone a real weapon. Christ all friggin mighty," Akern howled, turned, and walked away.

Both instructors just shook their heads as Akern walked out of the Hall. "Get your shit together girls, and form up outside! We are going to the armory and God help anyone on the ranges because if you shoot like you march, we're all going to die!"

Chapter 19

The Base Armory was a very secure area. It had massive doors, no windows and MPs everywhere. The recruits lined up and went inside to find four more Corporals with clipboards calling their names to form up at a chosen wicket.

Tony could feel his pulse racing and his hands sweating as he moved to the wicket. The Corporal there spoke loudly "name and SIN Recruit!" Tony complied with the order and the Corporal handed him his very own FNC-1 Rifle. Tony was like a groom on his wedding day, seeing his bride for the very first time. It was beautiful he thought.

The Issuing Corporal told Tony to step back, shoulder the weapon and report outside to his instructor. Tony did as he was told. The weapon seemed heavy, about ten pounds he guessed. It wasn't something to complain about. He reported to the instructor and they formed up outside, waiting for the rest of the recruits to finish weapons issue.

Tony looked at Keith and he could see a big shit-eating grin on his face.

Corporal Miller marched them back to the barracks and told them to stand by their beds with their weapons.

They moved into the barracks and headed for their bed spaces. They had to pass Steve Langford's open locker which had its contents blown to the four corners of his bed space. He had forgotten to secure his locker after trading his work dress for combats and it had been fell upon by an unknown assassin.

Keith looked at him, standing in the middle of his mess. "Remember what you said Steve, don't sweat the little stuff." Corporal Willows came up behind Langford and had him stand to attention, "if you ever leave your locker unsecured when the weapon is in it I will march you off to jail! Is that clear, Recruit?" "Yes, Corporal," came the swift reply.

Willows told the Squad that they had ten minutes to look over their weapons then secure them in their lockers until told to bring them out. This did not mean "cocking the weapon," just inspect.

Everybody went crazy looking at everything on their weapon, barrel, stock, cocking handle, front site, and of course the weight of it and the smell of gun oil. It had been a great day. The day might have been over but their personal duties were next

The Corporal had found enough dust on top of Recruit Jones' locker to "plant potatoes" he said and the recruit was there to be a soldier, not a farmer.

Tony and the rat pack had cleaning, dusting, and ironing clothes for the next day ahead of them.

The guys were getting used to dusting, even though, until Cornwallis they had never done it before. Ironing was another story.

The first time Tony and Keith used a hot iron, scorch marks were everywhere. The clothing had to be replaced. Practice makes perfect was the rule to live by. Polishing your boots and pushups were next in line, as well as helping Steve get his locker back together before he could store his weapon.

Tony's garbage can was next. All six guys hit that can with a vengeance and before long, it was gleaming. It was getting close to "lights out" and Tony was lying on his bed, thinking about the first day back.

Chapter 20

Up before 0500 hours, like he'd never been away, Tony went about cleaning his work station before heading to breakfast. A quick breakfast found the pack back in the barracks making sure that everything was ready for inspection.

In they came, looking for recruits to pounce on. They did find a couple, but not in Red Squad. The question of the day from the instructors was "where's your weapon, Recruit?" The proper answer was "secure, in my locker Corporal."

With inspection complete, the instructors told their charges to remember to bring their NBC (Nuclear, Biological Chemical) Masks and chemical suits to the classroom. There was one last thing to do before the day began and that was Tony's garbage can inspection.

A loud noise could be heard from the instructor's office. "Recruit Simons, report to the office with your can!" Tony grabbed the can and reported to the office. "Recruit Simons, reporting as ordered, Corporal." Tony submitted the can for inspection and he went over it with a fine-toothed comb. He even smelled the damn thing. Tony got a passing grade and was told to return the can to the hut.

As Tony removed the can from the office, he realized he wasn't happy about putting the great looking can back in that shit-hole, but what could he do.

They marched over to the gym and ran laps for the first half hour, followed by a great game of murder ball and then the rope climb. Fanning didn't know how to climb a rope, but with some private instruction from the group, he managed to get to the top with minor difficulty. The instructor told them that the mile and a half run was a week away, so they had better start getting ready for it.

A quick shower and out the door they moved, marching toward the classroom and NBC training. Getting to their desks the group was told by Corporal Miller that the GSK (General Service Knowledge) Test would take place the next week and he expected everyone to pass. Tony leaned over to Keith and said "things are happening, man."

They were not prepared for what happened next. A Corporal ran quickly into the classroom, grabbed his throat, gasped, because there was a fine smoke coming from his uniform and passed out on the floor. "Well?" the instructor said. "What do you do now?"

There was no movement from anybody. They all just sat looking at the guy on the floor until Bagley yelled "Holy Shit," grabbed for his mask and yelled "gas, gas, gas!"

The entire class was caught off guard and panic set in, as they all grabbed for their masks. The instructor was looking at his wrist watch while the class panicked. "Stop!" he commanded. "Don't move." The Corporal walked slowly around the room, stopping in front of more than half the class. "You're dead, you're dead and you're dead," he said 13 times.

The class was in various degrees of masking but it was clear they did not get their masks on in the nine seconds required. Some guys were still trying to get it out of the bag, others fumbled with the straps and some tried to put it on backwards. The recruits that did get it on, didn't check for leaks or cry out "gas, gas, gas."

The funniest one was a recruit tearing his mask off his face, trying to breathe because he didn't take the plug out of the canister. The dead Corporal came back to life and left the room, shaking his head.

Miller went back to the front of the classroom and looked at the recruits saying "you've got to be shitting me. We just did this yesterday."

The next hour was a blur of masking drills and this time they were doing it with their eyes closed. Tony was sure he would never be caught off guard again.

Corporal Miller then gave them something that he had never done before, a ten minute break to de-stress.

The drills were over for the day but the recruits kept their masks close, just in case, trusting Corporal Miller wasn't a good idea. Miller then changed the pace of the training by spending time on questions for the up-coming GSK Test.

The guys were getting good at answering the questions so it calmed them down for the remainder of the class. It was nearing lunch time and the recruits were excited because along with the drill in the afternoon, they would start learning about their weapons.

Corporal Miller saw that the questions had loosened them up, so ten minutes before they were to leave, he introduced the recruits to the next day's lessons by sticking a needle into the wood that surrounded the chalk board. This got their attention immediately.

"Gentlemen," Miller said with an evil smile, "tomorrow we will learn about the effects of chemical weapons and you will counter these effects by injecting yourselves with an atropine injector," and with that he stuck another one in the door trim leading out of the classroom. "Have a nice day ladies."

The march to the Mess Hall was quiet, but not without incident. The Platoon marched down the left side of the road, and another course was marching up the right side. Corporal Miller saw this happening and shouted out in a clear voice "be proud 7247." He got an immediate response from the Platoon as they straightened up, stepped out and held their arms as straight as a board.

As the platoons passed each other, you could see that they both had straightened up and were marching more like real soldiers. Corporal Miller's Platoon couldn't help but feel a pride in each other, but what they didn't see was the smile on Corporal Miller's face as he moved them down the road. He would certainly let Corporal Willows know what he was witness to and how proud he was.

Lunch was a submarine sandwich, soup and some bad-ass pudding, but the rat pack didn't even notice because the conversation was about that damn big needle sticking in the doorway. "What the hell does he expect us to do with that?" Van Meter gasped. "Biggest damn pipe I ever saw" said

Fanning. "I think it cracked the wood in the doorway."
Further conversation included "do we have to stick that thing in our arms?"

The conversation about the needle continued until it was time to head back to the barracks and pick up their weapons. They would be heading for another larger room in their training building, Room 22; for weapons familiarization, care and cleaning.

Willows was there to greet them and tell the group that he had the pleasure of escorting them to the classroom and would try to entertain them for the next two hours. They picked up their weapons and formed up outside with Willows going up and down the ranks, showing them how to hold the FNC-1 on the march.

"Hold the pistol-grip in your right hand" he said. "Keep your right arm straight down to your side and swing your left arm straight out on the march. Start showing the Base how proud you are to be here."

Willows called the march and Tony could feel the weapon at his side. He looked around; the Platoon seemed different. Marching was different this time.

They got to the classroom and laid their weapons on the tables in front of them. Willows began his lecture, holding his weapon out in front of him. "This is your FNC-1, 7.62

mm rifle. This is the most important piece of equipment you will ever own. This weapon has been called 'The Right Arm of the Free World.' This weapon can save your life."

There wasn't a peep in the classroom for the next two hours as all eyes were on the instructor as he took the recruits through the characteristics, assembly, and safety precautions of the FNC-1. His lecture took the whole two hours and the recruits had a new found respect for their weapons. They would practice what they had learned in class in the barracks every night because morning inspection just got even harder.

Back to the barracks and weapons secured, the recruits found that for the most part, little damage was inflicted during their absence. A quick march over to the Drill Hall brought the Platoon face to face with Sergeant Akern again, complete with his pace stick under his arm.

The instructors were ordered to correct the recruits as they drilled and try to correct the mistakes on the fly as Akern moved them around the floor. The Sergeant called the cadence and marched the recruits completely around the Drill Hall once before Recruit Jones got out of step. "Get it together Jones! You're making your Squad look bad! Straighten out your arms, watch your spacing and don't anticipate the next move."

Round and round they went until the Sergeant brought them to a halt. The instructor caught Recruit Welding moving after the halt and yelled at him to stand still, calling him an idle little crow.

Another half hour went by and the recruits were getting better listening to the different drill movements that the Sergeant called. He moved them around one more time and during the wheel, or left turn, the lead outside man did not hear the turn and continued to march straight ahead until he crashed into the wall, as the recruits marched away from him.

Sergeant Akern had a cow and started to berate the recruit for not listening to him, but as he had his mouth open wide and the words started falling out, so did his upper denture. It hit the floor and rolled some distance away from him. It was almost impossible not to laugh but everyone held it together except for one sad soul. He broke out laughing and went down on one knee trying to get control.

Sergeant Akern burned holes into the recruit with his eyes and walked over to retrieve his denture. He cleaned it off and put it back in his mouth. He then stood to attention and dismissed all the recruits except laughing boy.

The instructors marched the Platoon back to the barracks, leaving Mr. Football to feel the Sergeant's rage.

He was drilled for hours and got back to the block one hour before lights out. The other recruits had the time to go over what they had learned in weapons' class earlier.

They cleaned every piece of their rifles and took them apart numerous times just to put them together again. It was something more they had to do, but they didn't seem to mind. They were getting back into a routine again and even getting better at it. They could hardly wait for the next day and the "needle."

Chapter 21

Mornings were about getting ready for inspections, including weapons inspections. Breakfast was all about watching new courses come in. This included courses that were entirely female, but the guys thought some of the young ladies looked tougher than some of the men.

The gym was now a welcome way to start the morning and Tony was really getting back in shape and looking forward to class. Tony started out doing laps under time to get ready for the mile and a half. He knew he had this run in the bag and he was sure the rest of his Squad was ready as well.

After laps, the instructor had them in the pool for the rest of the training period swimming laps or drown-proofing. Tony was having trouble thinking about the next set of lessons. They say that when you want to avoid something, it seems to come up even quicker. This was the case with Tony and this "needle thing." He had never given himself a needle before and he wasn't happy about starting now.

Sitting at his desk in the classroom, he looked around and could see that he was not alone in his fear. The guys were truly uneasy with what was about to happen.

Corporals Willows and Miller came into the classroom carrying two boxes which could only be the reason Tony was already sweating, the atropine injectors!

The instructor for this lesson was Miller. It would have been easier for the recruits if Miller wasn't smiling so damn much and saying "this is going to be a great lesson. You're going to love it."

It started off rather dry, but picked up steam as he went along. They discussed methods of decontamination and protection against nuclear warfare at great length. Decontamination of chemical weapons using a mitt was also discussed. There was also donning the mask and decontaminating the mask. Miller also talked about chemical hazard signs and things that were out of the ordinary. Tony was thinking to himself "like smoke coming off a dead guy's combats maybe?" He hated what was coming up. Miller smiled "and so ladies, comes your minute of fame. This is how this injector works. Remember, you have only nine seconds to get this done, or you will die."

He reached into the box and pulled out a green cylinder about four inches long and a half an inch in diameter. It had a cap on each end, one red and one green. Miller then said that the recruits had to place the red cap of the cylinder inside their inner thigh and push down on the green side. This would release a spring-loaded needle which would enter their thigh and release atropine. In this case, it was only saline water, but the needle was real.

The guys were wide-eyed and their mouths were dry and hanging open at the thought of that pipe jamming a needle in their legs. Miller continued "push the green top, hear the pop, wait ten seconds and then pull the needle out. Bend the needle over on the desk and hook it in your left combat pocket. It's as easy as that," he said.

The recruits were sweating bullets listening to this.

"For demonstration purposes, I will go first," Willows said. With that he took out an injector, put it on the inside of his thigh and pushed. You could hear the snap throughout the classroom. Guys were breathing heavy and sweating buckets. The instructors stood in front of the recruits in the first two rows of desks and said "let's go recruit."

Recruit Fanning looked like he was being asked to cut off his manhood. The instructor handed him an injector and told him to get to it. Fanning slowly picked up the injector and positioned it on his thigh. "Take a breath and let it happen," Willows was saying.

Fanning looked away and pushed, nothing happened. He took a breath and tried again, nothing. He looked at the instructor and said "the injector must be defective, Corporal." The instructor's response was immediate. "Bullshit Fanning grow some balls! Do you want to die?"

Willows took the injector from the recruit and immediately fired it into the desk in front of him. At that precise moment twenty recruits diverted their attention to their desks. There, in front of them was something they hadn't noticed before. The desks were covered in worm holes obviously put there during prior atropine classes!

"Works just fine," Willows said. "Now get on with it." Recruit Fanning took a few more deep breaths and tried another injector. Again nothing happened as he started pounding it against his thigh. "Christ on a cross, Fanning," Willows said. "You're messing up my lesson." Willows again took the needle from him and fired it into the desk. A look came over Fanning's face and he took the third injector, positioned it and fired. "Snap!" went the loud noise. The look on his face was priceless. "Now count to ten Recruit, and then pull it out!"

A very fast ten-count later, Fanning had the needle hanging from his pocket. If Tony hadn't known better, he would swear that Fanning had peed himself!

The instructors went down the aisles stopping at each recruit and at times getting the same results.

Keith actually had to get up and walk around the classroom after it was done, just to keep from passing out.

Recruit Jones took it like a man, "nothing to it," he said and smiled.

Tony was visibly shaken; they were getting closer to him. He was watching the recruits' faces as they took the needle. Tony was sure most of the guys saw god that morning. Then, his time came; Miller was in front of Tony holding out an injector. "This one's got your name on it Simons." All the blood drained from Tony's face and his hands were ice-cold.

He took what he thought looked like a large pipe, and stared at it for a second or so. "Well," Miller said, looking at his face. Tony then placed the huge pipe on his inner thigh, took a breath and pushed. Nothing happened. Miller was taking the injector from him and sticking it in the desk.

"Stop being a little girl," he said and gave him another. Tony placed it and pushed. There was a snap and what he thought was the worst pain he had ever felt. "Count to ten Recruit, and get this done." Miller said. Tony pulled the needle out and looked at it. His eyes widened. It looked as large as a drinking straw for Christ's sake! He bent the needle on the desk and hung it on his pocket before starting to breath.

He wasn't the last one to take the needle. There were many souls that were going to go through the same horror he had just experienced.

Tony looked at the clock, 1200 hours! It was over and Willows called them a bunch of babies before releasing them for lunch.

Very few of the recruits could eat. They were still in shock about what had just happened. They all talked about the size of the needle. Each one of them prayed that they would never be put in a situation where they would have to do that for real.

Chapter 22

A quick march to the barracks to pick up their weapons was good for their sore legs and they were off to the Drill Hall for the afternoon.

The recruits were given a class on their weapons and then drill began, this time with their weapons.

They spread out on the floor with their FNC-1 in front of them and Corporal Miller went over what they had learned the day before along with the day's lesson; holding, aiming, firing, immediate action drills and stoppages. They were allowed to break down the rifle and then re-assemble it. Miller said that this was important because at some point they would have to do it in the dark. Miller also began to show them how to shoot standing up, kneeling and lying down.

This went on for two hours and everybody was coming up to speed. They took a 10-minute break then formed up in three ranks with their weapons. Sergeant Akern arrived and took over the lesson. He showed the recruits how to carry a rifle while marching, along with other movements.

"This is the type of drill that you will be required to do at the Friday graduation parades from now on, ladies. By the time you get to your graduation, you'll be much better at it, if you're lucky enough to get there."

The recruits picked up on this remark right away. It was the first time graduation had ever been mentioned. Thus far, for the Friday graduation parades, the guys had not been carrying weapons.

They got used to moving with the weapon and weren't doing badly, even as the Sergeant was growling at them every other minute. Tony liked marching with his weapon and concentrated on the commands, trying not to mess up. The lesson was almost over, but you could see that Akern was getting more and more annoyed with a recruit named Butler. He was one of the recourse recruits that had arrived that week and was having trouble staying in step.

Butler was having trouble with drill. Standing still he was fine but as soon as he started to march, he was immediately out of step; or, as the Sergeant called it, bear-walking. This is while marching his left arm followed his left leg and the right side, the same. This drove Akern crazy, but he knew how to fix it. It was called pace-stick marching.

He had Butler take one end of the Sergeant's pace stick and had the recruit in front of Butler grab the other end so they were connected. They were told to hold onto the ends as they marched. Butler would be forced to be in step as they moved. It worked like a charm. Tony had more respect for the wise old Sergeant after that.

Back in the barracks at the end of the day the rat pack got together and talked about the day as they shined their shoes and stripped their weapons. Some were trying to do it blind-folded and found it difficult.

Lying on his bed after lights out, Tony kept hearing the old Sergeant's voice over and over in his head "this is how you do it when you graduate;" as he fell asleep.

Chapter 23

Friday was the same as Thursday with the difference being that they weren't jamming a pipe into their legs. The drills were coming easier and the marching cleaner. Even Butler was doing better with his drill. Miller tried to catch the group with a gas call, but the Squad was wise to him and passed with flying colors.

The Squad was getting very excited when the day ended. They knew that they would be going to the Green and Gold that night to have a beer. Corporal Willows reminded the Squad to be on their best behavior and not to embarrass the course in any way.

Being confined to barracks was lifted and the recruits were allowed to go to the CANEX and shop or just get away from the rest of the Platoon. They could even order in now, if the mess food was getting too hard to handle. They thought it was like being in heaven.

Supper that night was a blur and the pack got back to the barracks to clean up and wait for the Green and Gold to open. Their dress had to be S3 or full Military dress and the guys looked fine, all decked out and shiny.

2000 hours came and the rat pack entered the doors of the famous Green and Gold Bar. They could smell alcohol immediately and hear the din of many conversations of many courses. The place was filling up fast but the pack found a table and settled in. Looking around they saw trophies and pictures of military guns and airplanes as well as ships.

It was green everywhere and the bar was like Tony had never seen before. It was oak and brass and glass. Keith got up and went to get the first round of beers for the table. He said hello to the bartender and was about to take out his ID. "Not necessary," the bartender said. "If you're old enough to serve, you're old enough to be served."

Keith didn't know any names of the beers they were selling. On the list were beers like "10 Penny, Five Star, Moosehead, and Old Vienna." He was even more amazed that the cost of the beer was only 25 cents.

Keith finally chose Old Vienna for the group and once back at the table, everyone stood up and toasted the course and congratulated each other for making it this far.

The first beer was history in no time flat. The second and subsequent beers went down slowly because the table was a mad-house of conversation about the instructors, the other guys in the Platoon, Christmas Holidays and what would be coming up in the "field exercises."

Tony said that he had never been so lucky as to know friends like the ones seated at the table, and he hoped they would be pals forever. The evening was over way too soon and the guys made it back to the barracks. The marching was slightly inhibited by alcohol. When they got back they sat in the TV room, more relaxed than they had been in quite some time. They still had the rest of the weekend ahead of them.

Saturday morning found the barracks just about deserted and not having to get up at 0500 hours was quite different, and not being on a schedule was exciting.

Tony shook Keith out of bed and they hurried down to the mess for Saturday breakfast, consisting of pancakes, sausages and toast. Then they went down to the CANEX to look at people other than the guys on their course. This was hard to do because half the course was already there.

Tony and Keith walked in to see women, real young ladies, decked out in military uniforms, but girls just the same. The guys walked around the CANEX for quite some time before stopping to have a burger and fries; it had been a really long time.

They bought a few personal items, like boot polish and Tony found some black licorice, his favourite treat. He'd keep this in his kit box, in the lower level, because that's where his private stuff was.

Before heading back to the barracks, they stopped at the local information board just to see what was going on. There was typical stuff on the board; Bake Sale, Lost and Found, along with stuff for sale and fast food menus for ordering in. "Ordering in," said Tony, "what a concept." He looked at Keith and said "we can do that now." He wrote down a couple of numbers that delivered burgers, and fried chicken. There was also a pizza place called "The Hollow Spot."

Back to the barracks they marched, much happier with the small amount of freedom and a place they could get a burger.

Once back, Tony stashed his licorice away in his kit-box, not really paying attention to anything when Keith came up behind him. "What's that Tony?" Keith asked. Tony realized that he was looking at Betty's drawing that he had taken out of the box and inadvertently placed on his bed.

Tony looked up quickly and snatched the picture off the bed to return it to the box before he answered. He looked at

Keith, smiled and told him that the drawing was given to him by someone he was very fond of and the drawing was important to him. Keith wanted to know more. He knew Tony had a story he wasn't telling, but he was sure that they would sit down one night and Tony would let him in.

The Green and Gold Bar was on the agenda for Saturday night and again the conversation was lively.

The weekend was totally relaxing and before they knew it, it was Sunday night. Corporal Willows came in at about 2100 hours and reminded the recruits that the next day would start a busy week six so they best be on their toes because they would be going through the Gas Hut soon!

Chapter 24

Monday morning of week six saw the recruits in the gym, running, and doing pushups and sit-ups. They were getting ready for the mile and a half run on Friday. Even the PERI had to admit they were in good shape, but of course he wouldn't out loud.

Classroom training consisted of more weapons' familiarization on a new gun called the FNC-2 which was a modification of the FNC-1 with a tripod. Next was the Sterling C-1 Sub-Machine Gun. Safety precautions, as well as strip and assembly, load, hold, aim and fire were all covered in great detail. Basically, the Sub-Machine Gun was just a pipe with a magazine attached to it. You put the mag in, pull the trigger and the thing goes nuts.

Everyone knew the C-1 weapon as "the plumber's nightmare." Miller and Willows went over and over all the ways these weapons worked and then went over them again. The time zoomed by.

After a short break the recruits moved right into mask training and decontamination. They had the drills down pat but getting in and out of the suit was a little tricky and took a lot of practice. The next day they would write the test and the following week they would enter the Gas Hut.

The rest of the morning was spent going over the questions they would see on the NBC test along with mask drills and weapons drill.

The afternoon found the recruits with their weapons in the Drill Hall being trained on how to properly salute or "pay compliments." Up to now, they didn't have to salute officers or the flag because they were not yet trained. This day that would end and after the class they would be compelled to salute when necessary. It wasn't a hard lesson, but it put added responsibility on the recruits to show respect.

The next day, after final preparations, the recruits sat down in their classroom to write their tests on NBC. They were a little nervous at first because they had to pass or they would not be allowed to enter the Gas Hut. To Tony's surprise, everyone finished early and the guys were slapping each other on the back coming out of the test room. Tony had no doubt that he had aced the test.

It seemed to the recruits, that the instructors were concentrating on drill and the need for the recruits to be on top of their game as the drill test came closer. Weapons drill was taking on a new meaning and the Sergeant was making sure that everybody understood his commands. This afternoon they were practicing standing rifle drill and weapons saluting. Simply done, the weapon is moved to the front of the body and the left hand slaps the magazine to complete the move.

Tony and Keith had practiced this move many times in barracks and were looking really good. However, fate has a habit of stepping in and messing things up when you don't want it to. The command was given and Recruit Van Meter moved his weapon forward and slapped the magazine. The bottom of the magazine let loose and the clip and spring popped out of the weapon and sprung out on the floor like a slinky.

Van Meter had a heart attack and the rest of the Platoon broke out laughing uncontrollably. Even the Sergeant's jaw dropped and he turned away from the group to compose himself. The rest of the training went without incident, thank god.

Tony was always busy and had little time for himself during the week. It was good, though, because being busy kept his mind off what was happening. He was getting closer to graduation. That meant he was going to start his new career, his new life! How great was that!

Friday finally came and the recruits were excited to get the mile and half run out of the way. They dressed in track suits, toques and mitts because even though it was milder, they still had to stay warm. They were given the opportunity of running indoors but they refused, so out they went.

Corporal Dane had already shown them the course they were to take and was about to turn them loose. They were like nervous race horses, just before the gate opens.

Corporal Dane told them he would see them at the finish and that he was sure they would all make it.

Off they went, nervous yells of "let's go, and come on" were heard, but Tony was inside himself and planning the next 12 minutes. Some of the guys burst out running at full speed at the start, screaming as they went by him. Tony knew this was a mistake and he moved out at a steady pace watching his breath.

All in all it was a nice morning, but there was a chill in the air. Groups of guys ran together and some alone. Tony, Keith and Steve ran together, pacing each other. "How are you doing Keith," Tony called. "I'm with you man," he replied. At the half way mark Steve complained that his legs were burning so he slowed his pace.

They started to pass guys that were slowing down because they started too fast. Tony gave them encouragement as he ran by telling them to concentrate.

When he was almost at the finish Tony was feeling the pain but the three kept encouraging each other. Tony was starting to panic. He was cold and wanted to stop in order to catch his breath. He heard a tired Keith yelling in his ear to keep moving. Tony started doubting himself and then thought about why he was here and what he had to do to get to the finish line. One last deep breath and Tony thundered down the street to the finish line, crossing with his arms out like a long-distance runner finishing 26 miles. This was one hell of a way to start the day was all he could think about.

He looked back and the rat pack was all around him. Corporal Dane was checking times as the recruits crossed the finish line and confirmed that they had all made the time. The recruits had the rest of the period to swim, shower and get ready for the next class.

Once in the classroom, the instructors took the group through weapons drill once again and this time they were given timed competitions to see who could strip and assemble their weapons the fastest.

They were taught about service ammunition and the need to be safe around it at all times. Willows started talking to them about "field living," and using "bush craft tools." "Field living" means building a fire, cooking rations and constructing a shelter or "hooch" as he called it. Tony could sense a change in the instruction and how the instructors were presenting the lectures. They seemed to be more interested in making sure they understood rather than focusing on ripping their faces.

They went on to talk about hygiene and sanitation, both very important in the bush. They talked about the compass and how to read a map. They stressed being able to camouflage and conceal yourself.

The recruits knew they were going into the bush soon and they could hardly wait.

All in all it had been a very good week, but Tony was looking forward to a beer and getting away for the weekend. He had a Leave Pass and he was going to use it!

Chapter 25

The pack had already decided that getting away, even if only to the nearest town would be a good idea. At the end of the day they all cleaned and showered, got into their finest uniforms and marched to the gate and the waiting taxi. They piled in and had the driver take them to Brown's Cove, down the road about an hour away to the "Old Man of the Sea Inn," which they had booked a few days earlier. It was great to be away with just the pack.

When they arrived they piled into the cabin and they found it did indeed sleep six, but it was much like the barracks. Tony loved it and scored a bed near the window looking out onto the Cove. It didn't take long for the guys to unpack and head for the local liquor store.

It was small and tidy but six thirsty recruits can mess things up really quick while moving bottles around and looking for things to buy. The old man at the till knew where the guys were from and smiled to himself because he had seen this sort of thing many times before.

Tony and the pack bought a lot of beer and liquor and anything else they could get their hands on.

Back in the room they opened many bottles and drank many beers while talking about the course and graduating soon.

They ordered in from the local chicken place and settled in for the night.

Tony was mellowing out and he was finding out more and more stuff about his friends that he did not know. Ron Van Meter did live real close to Port Nichols, two miles to be precise. They knew some of the same people and had probably gone to the same schools. Ron liked to shoot pool and had played at John's Pool Hall a time or two.

Keith was another story; he had grown up just outside Saskatoon, on a farm but did most of his socializing in "Toon Town" as he called it. School was a drag for him and his dad was not getting any younger and he wanted Keith to do more and take over at some point. Keith knew that it was time to get out while the getting was good.

Steve Langford was from a small town just north of Edmonton, Alberta. He was the oldest son of a couple of hippy parents that spent most of their youth high and playing in rock bands. They were on the road a lot playing gigs so Steve looked after his two younger sisters until they were old enough to look after themselves and here he was.

Rick Bagley was from a northern Ontario town called "Bozen." It had a population of 350 hard working souls that worked in the logging industry, in a mill. The mill was the only industry in the area, so if you wanted a job it was in the mill or the local grocery store. The school was one classroom that taught five grades. After that you had to bus twenty miles to the bigger town of "Northern Pines" to finish high school. Rick told the guys he couldn't see himself working in the mill next to his mother and father for the rest of his life. When he saw an ad on TV for the military, he jumped at it.

The last of the group was Ken Fanning, Fanny for short or Mr. Handsome as he preferred to be called. He was from Halifax. It was an easy call for Mr. Handsome. His grandfather was army, his father was army and Mr. Handsome was going to follow the family tradition and be a ground-pounder or what the guys called a "hole technician." He could hardly wait to show his dad what he looked like in uniform with an "Army" cap badge on his hat and not a "cornflake."

"What's your story, Tony?" Bagley asked. "What brings you here, buddy?" The group all looked at Tony and waited for his reply. Tony shrugged and shook his head "nothing exciting here guys. I'm a small town boy, moved around some and didn't want to work in a winery all my life. That's my story, no drama."

The story passed muster with most of the group, but Tony saw Keith looking at him and knew that he was going to have to confide in his friend before much longer.

Ron was getting pleasantly loaded by then and was quite happy with his chicken when a light came on in his foggy brain. "It was Friday night! What does a small town do on a Friday night?"

Steve was crushing a beer can and launching it into a garbage can across the room. He looked up and asked "do they have a Legion?" All the guys sat up and looked at the big recruit lying on the couch. "That's brilliant!" Rick piped up, and showered Steve with an open bag of potato chips.

It was about 2100 hours when the guys walked through the door of what was the only Legion in a 50 mile radius, so this was the area hotspot. The room was near filled to capacity with dart players, locals and vets from all the wars. Tables were loud with conversation. The guys walked in, and were greeted warmly and told to grab a table and have fun.

Tony looked around and could see that this was the place to be on a Friday night. There were dart boards up on the wall, pool tables to the side and shuffle board was being played everywhere. Everyone was having a great time.

The boys settled in and were having a few beers, trying to decide if pool was their game of choice when Steve said he thought he heard music coming from upstairs. He went to the bar and asked the bartender what was going on and was told a local band was jamming upstairs and a dance was taking place.

This got the guys excited and after a few more bottles of courage, they went up the stairs into the dance hall. The lights were a little on the low side, but Tony could see that they were probably the youngest people in the room. The band wasn't that great and their choice of music was not what the recruits were used to listening to, but it seemed that the people there liked it and they filled the floor, moving around wildly to the beat.

Tony and the pack were in cougar country and they knew it! The average age of the ladies there were beyond 35 or more and none were that good looking. They also out-numbered the men by two to one.

The cougars targeted the young men as soon as they came into the room and it wasn't long after that the boys were laughing and dancing with the ladies and having a hell of a good time. These ladies knew how to party! After many shots of whiskey and a few slow dances, the groups paired off and were in separate corners of the dance hall.

Tony had gotten together with an older lady named "Marilyn." She was divorced with two kids and worked at the corner store. She was there to have a good time and that was all. This was an awesome relief to Tony because he had never been hit on so fast and wasn't sure how it was going to end up.

More booze, more dancing and the evening ended. The ladies thanked the recruits for a great time and the guys got back together to swap stories and call a cab.

Keith looked around at the guys and noticed that one of them was missing. "Where the hell is Steve?" he said. Everyone was shaking their heads and trying to remember when they last saw him. There were plenty of answers. He was seen at the bar, in the washroom and on the dance floor.

Tony remembered him dancing with an older lady with curly black hair, heavy makeup and a jean vest. He was looking really happy. Tony went to the bar and asked the bartender if he had seen his friend leave the dance hall and whether or not he was alone.

Merle, the bartender, nodded his head and said that Steve had left the hall with the town's school principal and they were looking pretty cozy. All Tony could say was "really?" He went back to the group and told them that Steve had been picked up by the school's principal and chances of finding him tonight were pretty slim. "Let's get back to the room and have a drink. He'll find his way back in the morning," Tony said. "He's a big boy."

Everyone was laughing and shaking their heads as the cab came and took them back to their room. Everyone had a few more beers and talked about the loss of their compadre to a hungry cougar when they weren't looking.

The guys finally woke in the early afternoon and then spent most of their time holding their heads and wishing they had not drank so much.

They eventually sauntered down to the local restaurant for food and more conversation as to what had happened the night before and the fact that Steve was still missing in action.

"Don't sweat it," Fanny said. "He knows where we are and when we are leaving."

The group decided to look around the town and around the cove before heading back to the room to decide what they were going to do that evening. Everyone agreed they needed supplies like: chips, pop, pork rinds, and something to make a sandwich out of. The corner store was the next location to be found. It was easy and the guys entered the store laughing and pushing each other like guys do.

They scattered out to find what they needed and returned to the till, surprised to be eye to eye with Marilyn from the night before. Tony recognized her right away and she smiled at him when she remembered his face. "Thanks for last night," she said. "You were a real gentleman." "My pleasure Marilyn," Tony said. "It was a lot of fun." She looked at him and said "I hear you lost a member of your group last night." Tony was shocked that Marilyn knew this. She shrugged and looked at him and said "small town." Word got around quickly that Sally Martin was seen hauling a young uniformed man into her apartment at about 3:00 o'clock that morning and she hadn't surfaced yet. It was an easy guess that he was one of your group after watching Sally sink her claws into him on the dance floor.

Tony laughed a bit and thanked Marilyn for the information and told her that if she saw him to send him home.

Outside, Tony told the pack what he had heard and that the whole town knew what was going on. All he got from the guys was "holy shit."

Saturday evening found Tony and the pack, minus Steve, at a local pub having a seafood dinner and a drink or two. They all agreed that they would have to find Steve the next day because it would soon be home time and the fun was over. They closed the pub around 0200 hours and made it back to the room to find the lights on along with the TV and Steve, dead drunk sitting on the toilet with his head in his hands.

Keith laughed loudly as Steve raised his head and they could see a huge hickey on his neck. "I'm going to die," was all he said. He then headed to the couch to pass out. "Don't talk to me, I've got nothing to say," was all they got and then he went to sleep.

Everybody was laughing their ass off as they toasted their hero who had taken on a cougar and survived to talk about it.

The next morning involved a quick shower, shave and a coffee; getting dressed and calling a cab to head back to the Base. Steve was still not talking, but the guys were not going to leave him alone anytime soon.

Chapter 26

Getting ready for week seven was easy, combats all day, every day, except Thursday. It would be course photos at the end of that day. They were getting to the end of the training and it was time to have their pictures taken looking military.

The guys in the rat pack teased Steve unmercifully and told him his hickey was going to get real dark come Thursday and no amount of makeup was going to cover it. There was a bet between the recruits as to whether or not Corporal Willows would spot it and what he would say.

Dress greens were turned into the Base Drycleaner for pressing on Monday morning so that everyone would look their best for Thursday.

The morning was easy, gym was a snap and most of the recruits did pushups and sit-ups before hitting the pool to cool off. During some water treading time Tony found himself near Steve and he looked at him and said "well

Steve, are you going to tell me or not?" "Not," Steve replied swiftly.

"You have to confess at least to me, buddy. They won't leave you alone and you know it," Tony pushed back. "If you don't tell me, I'm going to make something horrible up and make sure that little shit Bennett knows about it. You know he can't keep a secret. It'll be around the whole course, including the instructors by lunch."

Steve floated over to the side of the pool and put his head down on his hands before he began. "She used me, Tony; she used me and told me to lock the door on my way out. She kept biting my ear and grabbing my ass on the dance floor. I couldn't believe she was a school principal! She whispered in my ear that we should get out of there and go to her place that wasn't far. It sounded like a plan to me and she wasn't that old. We got to her place and as soon as the door closed, she slammed me up against the wall and started grabbing my goods. We didn't even get the lights on, for Christ's sake. She pulled me into a dark bedroom and pushed me onto the bed. She somehow got my pants off in the dark and was on me like a crazed animal. I still had my shirt and tie on and she was riding the hell out of me.

It was so dark in there, I couldn't see a thing. It went on for a long time and I was beginning to wonder if she was going to run out of steam. It seemed to me there was no way in hell she was getting off me. It was breaking dawn because I could see a sliver of light coming in through the darkened window. She finally rolled off and passed out and I don't remember a thing. I just shut down. I woke up at about three in the afternoon to the smell of coffee and bacon and the sound of a radio playing. I went into the kitchen and she turned, smiled and said "that was a hell of a night! Did you sleep well?" She smiled and confessed that it had been a while since she had been with anyone and hoped she wasn't too aggressive.

Steve told Tony that, for an old gal, she still looked pretty good. After having something to eat, Sally told Steve that the shower was his if he wanted to freshen up. "I knew I needed the shower, Tony, so I went in and turned on the water. The hot water felt good and it cleared my head a bit, but as I started to wash my goods, the shower curtain pulled back and there she was."

Tony looked at his friend, "did she at least let you wash?" he asked. Steve smiled back at him and said "we washed everything, buddy, wound up back in bed and this time I was on top. It was late when I woke up and she was still sleeping. I cleaned up, dressed and was going to say goodbye when she rolled over and said 'you let yourself out lover and thanks'!"

Tony looked shocked and said "that's it?" "That's it," Steve replied. "I went out the door and went down to a small pub for a few rums to get my head straight and then I came back to the room."

"When did you get that bite on your neck, Steve?" All Tony got in return was Steve shaking his head.

The classroom was abuzz about Steve's monster hickey and the mystery around how he got it. He wasn't talking so only guesses could be made, along with a lot of chuckling.

Corporal Miller came into the classroom and threw something into the air that had been hidden in his hand. It was white powder and it filled the air around them. The class reacted immediately and went for their masks. Less than nine seconds later they were all yelling "gas, gas, gas." Corporal Miller went around looking for incorrect fitting masks and seals. He was also looking for anything out of the ordinary.

He knew that the recruits had been away for the weekend and he was damn sure if any of them were hung over, they were going to pay. The recruits were all standing up with their masks on as Corporal Miller walked down the aisle, looking at everyone. He passed Steve and stopped in his tracks. He backed up and stopped in front of the recruit and stared closely at his hickey for some time before asking him "did you get into a fight this weekend Recruit Langford?"

"No Corporal," was Steve's muffled reply. "Well, then did someone punch you in the neck?" "No Corporal," was another muffled reply. Miller stood back waiting for the recruit to explain. "Rat bite," was the reply. "You've got big damn rats in Nova Scotia, Corporal."

Miller blinked many times. "Did you at least get a chance to bite her back?" he asked. "Many times, Corporal Miller, many times."

Miller walked away saying "carry on Recruit."

Steve was happy that it was finally lunch time, after which the Squad found themselves back in the barracks picking up their weapons and they were about to head to the Drill Hall. Tony was closing his locker when a bellow was heard from the Instructor's office. "Recruit Simons get your ass in here now!"

Tony felt like he was just hit with a hammer. A million things went through his head, trying to find that one thing he did wrong, that would bring these animals down on his head. They already had one casualty. Recruit Fanning had to march to the office and explain why the bartender had taken away his bar card and suspended his drinking privileges the week before. That didn't go well for Fanning. They were not giving it back to him, ever. Now it was Tony's turn.

When a recruit is called to the office, there is protocol that must be followed. You knock on the door and wait. When you get permission to enter, you step through the door, close it, and take three paces forward and come to attention.

Corporals Miller and Willows were sitting behind their desks looking at the recruit and shaking their heads. Corporal Willows started in on Tony like he was some kind of criminal. "What the hell is with you, Simons?" Tony was thunderstruck. What did he do?

He didn't move and he didn't speak. Willows went on. "Do you think that you're not watched 24/7? Nothing comes into this Base that isn't checked and double-checked to see that no drugs or pornographic material gets through. We weed out these types of assholes and perverts so as not to hurt the other recruits and the training that goes on here. Am I getting through to you, Recruit Simons?" Corporal Willows was standing now.

Tony's heart was racing and he was beginning to sweat. "Is he saying I'm a drug dealer?" Tony thought. "Are they throwing me out?" he panicked. Miller reached into his desk, took out what looked like a letter and put it on the desk in front of Tony.

"What the hell is this, Simons? Pick it up and look at it." Miller's voice was getting louder. Tony picked up the letter and to his surprise, noticed it was addressed to him. "What the hell," he thought. The writing on the envelope was child-like and the address barely correct. What stood out the most were a hand-drawn choo choo train on the back and skull and crossbones on the envelope seal. Across it was printed "get this to Tony fast and keep it away from the military police."

Tony thought he was going to faint. He knew by the printing that Dick had written the letter and was trying to be funny in his own sick little way.

"Do you know who this is?" Willows demanded.

Tony answered the question quietly, trying not to shake. "It's from my old man, Corporal Willows, he's an asshole."

Tony was ordered to open the envelope and hand it to the instructor. Willows read the letter quickly and handed it to Miller. "Is your old man an idiot, Simons?" he asked. "Did he think this would not be stopped?" Miller handed the letter back to Tony and he quickly read the one-page scrawl. It was Dick alright. The letter was short and badly written, but Tony got the point right away.

"I heard you were in town and you didn't bother to come home!" Dick scrawled. "No big deal, though, just thought you might see your way clear to send us a couple of bucks. I'll try to get it back to you when I can." It was signed "Dick."

Tony explained his relationship with his dead-beat father to the instructors and said in no uncertain terms that he would never send this man any money.

Tony apologized to the instructors for Dick's stupidity and asked them to please tear up the letter. Willows agreed to destroy the letter and said that he would not make a note on his file. Tony came to attention, turned and left the office. "That son of a bitch," he said under his breath and he grabbed his rifle and made his way to the street and the waiting platoon.

Rifle drill, or what the recruits were calling, graduation drill, went perfectly; and the Sergeant was telling them that their drill test was coming up soon and he was sure they would do well. He also said that they could not slack off or get sloppy. He told them that their Ten Mile Run/March was the following week as well, so they would need more time in the gym on the track. This run would be with full pack, helmets, and rifles and would test them to their core.

The time went quickly and the recruits were given more down time. The weapons familiarization with the FN and the Machine Gun were completed with little effort. They were getting close, and they knew it.

The next day was Gas Hut training day and the recruits had no idea what to expect. The training would be all afternoon, hands on and the Squad was expected to man-up and get it done the first time.

They hit the gym in the morning and took the Sergeant's advice about training more on the track. All but ten minutes was spent running and the guys put some time into pushups and sit-ups. The PERI didn't bother them much, he was there mainly to supervise now and make sure things were done correctly.

The pool was wonderful and the next class was just reviewing GSK and what they would be doing in the Hut that afternoon.

Their lunch was light with the recruits only having a sandwich or two and a glass of milk or juice. No sense loading up if you stood a chance of throwing it back up.

Back in the barracks they gathered up their masks and formed up outside, readying themselves for a march to the far side of the Base and the Gas Hut. They were surprised to see that the instructors had ordered a truck to transport them to the Hut, but they would be marching back. It wasn't a long ride, but the recruits appreciated it.

Chapter 27

They arrived at the Gas Hut to find not what they expected. It wasn't a huge black building with bars on the windows and old gas masks and kit lying around in front. Instead they found a simple 20 by 10 wooden shack with windows on both sides and a door painted green. There was fencing around the building for safety purposes. It would keep people that were passing by from getting too close and being exposed to lingering CS gas.

They piled out of the truck and while Corporal Miller stayed with the troops outside, Corporal Willows donned his mask and entered the building carrying a small can. "When you get inside you might feel a slight stinging in your eyes and throat," Corporal Miller said. "That will be from residual CS from other courses. Don't panic and whatever you do, don't rub your eyes."

They went through the door with their masks in their bags and tried not to breathe at all or open their eyes more than a slit, but you have to. You have to see, you have to breathe.

Tony got into the Hut and did the same as everybody else until he took a deep breath and opened his eyes more. To his surprise it wasn't bad. He could feel a burning on his lips but that was all.

Corporal Willows, on the other hand, was taking no chances. He was masked up tight as he fired up a hot plate. "Listen up Squad," he said. "When this gets hot, I'm going to add CS gas pellets to the pan and they will melt down quickly. The gas will be in the form of a cloud and you will definitely know when it hits you."

The guys spread out along the walls in the room and the room began to fill with CS gas. Thick smoke was everywhere. Willows had them doing calisthenics to get their bodies warmed up and the sweat starting. Everyone was feeling the effects of the gas in different ways but one thing was the same, the burning and stinging pain in their eyes as they began to tear up.

Tony was trying not to breath too much but Corporal Willows had them recite their SIN and name in the gas-filled room and that got things happening. Even after being warned, the guys were rubbing their eyes and the stinging needle pain got even worse. They bolted for the door only to find Miller on the other side washing their eyes out with a canteen and sending them back into the gas.

Willows yelled "gas, gas, gas!" and the recruits finally grabbed their masks, and had them on in record time. They blew air out after getting their masks on to ensure that the gas had not entered the mask while they removed it from their bags. Some didn't blow the air and paid the price of breathing in CS gas. They puked in their masks and ripped it from their faces.

Outside they ran in terror only to find Miller with a canteen of water to clean the mask and send them back in. Everyone had been sweating and the gas burned everything that was wet; throat, eyes, armpits, and of course the crotch area. Tony's only saving grace was that he got his mask on properly the first time and was watching the horror show that was going on around him. It seemed to go on forever he thought, until he finally heard Corporal Willows order them outside. He told them not to touch their eyes no matter what.

Miller was at the door when they exited and told them to leave the masks on and get into the open to pat themselves down. "Try not to get down-wind from anybody else because you could get gassed again when you take your mask off."

Tony thought that was the best advice he had heard all day and looked for a clear spot while beating on his combats.

Corporal Willows came out of the Hut, looked around at the recruits and called "gas clear."

The men removed their masks, and were clearing their eyes with water when Willows piped up "who wants to go again? We have all day to play." There were of course, no takers.

Bagley had puked in his mask and was in the process of cleaning it out when Tony walked over to him to see if he was ok. "That's enough fun for today, hey Rick?" he said. Rick looked up at him with red swollen eyes, "no shit," was all he could get out.

Marching back to the barracks gave the guys a chance to air out their combats and feel the cool clean breeze on their faces. Every now and then Tony got a whiff of the gas coming off someone's combats, but it quickly went away.

The march took about half an hour, but it was the best they felt all day. They had beat the dreaded Gas Hut and lived to tell about it!

Chapter 28

Back in the barracks' TV room that night, they talked without end about their experiences in the horrible Hut until it was lights out. Tomorrow would be a new day.

They say there is always calm before a storm and Wednesday morning came a storm called Corporal Willows. Morning inspection should have gone on without a hitch. They had had plenty of practice with the inspection stuff. That was not the case. Corporal Willows was moving down the row of open lockers when he stopped unexpectedly at the locker of a recruit named Grassley.

Tony didn't know him that well. He was okay to talk to but he mainly stayed to himself. Willows was looking in his locker and telling him what a fine locker layout he had and that he should be proud of himself. The praise stopped suddenly as Willows stopped and touched something in Grassely's locker and yelled! "What the Christ is this Grassely? What the hell do you think you're getting away with? How long has this been going on, you waste of space?"

Tony glanced at Van Meter and got that "I don't know" look from him. It didn't take long to find out what Grassely had been up to, as Van Meter and Tony began to see underwear sailing by and hitting the wall. Normally this wouldn't have been newsworthy but the underwear hit the wall and stayed in its 4 x 4 configuration. More underwear sailed by, then a shirt and a towel and finally sock hotdogs. Willows was destroying Grassely's locker. It would seem that Grassely had spray-starched most of his kit until it was solid so he wouldn't have to continuously iron it. They were in fact solid puzzle pieces that looked great from a distance, but up close you could see the difference and Willows was definitely up close.

Willows put Grassely on report and gave him extra duties for the remainder of the week, but that was not the end of the storm. Corporal Willows was a man possessed. He yelled for Miller and together, they went through everyone's locker, grabbing stuff and throwing it all over the barracks.

The barracks was a shit-pit, but they did find two others that were in on the scam with Grassely. It truly was a shitty way to start the day, after which Corporal Willows gave everyone in the barracks extra duties. He said that they were supposed to be a team and if one man screwed up it was because the team didn't see it or chose to look away; therefore they were all at fault.

Tony looked at his destroyed bed space and locker and was not impressed at all. He would talk to Grassely at the end of the day and remind him about the team thing. The mess that the instructors caused was left where it was and the Squad went off to run the track and do floor exercises.

While the guys were getting into their gym clothes, they too were thanking Grassely for being such an asshole and causing so much shit this late in their training.

The instructor had them set up a game of murder ball and much to no one's surprise, Grassely was the main target.

Classroom time was spent on GSK questions and the instructors added a twist to them by getting the recruits to answer ten questions in a row before moving to the next man. During the last half hour Corporal Miller talked to them about Exercise Grandville Ferry where the Platoon would be spending two days and two nights in the bush. He didn't go into detail but he said that it was one of the best times he had ever had and they would think so too.

They were dismissed to lunch but instead of losing that half hour they decided to march back to the barracks and begin trying to clean up the mess that was waiting for them, Corporal Miller agreed.

Corporal Willows took charge after and marched them over to the Drill Hall but before he started the practice he gave them a briefing on what was expected of them during their drill test and of course the upcoming graduation parade.

The drill test would be administered by the School's Second in Command, and they would be required to go through all of their drill movements with accuracy and determination. "If someone makes a mistake," Willows said, "don't move and draw attention to the mistake. Just continue on. Listen and work together and you will pass."

They needed to show the officers that this platoon knew what they were doing. The graduation parade would be all pomp and ceremony. Every course that was presently being trained would be included in the parade and 7247 would be front and center facing the Base Commander. This realization unnerved Tony a little, thinking that his Squad was going to be watched by the whole Base. They would be in full military dress, complete with white gloves, white belts and silver bayonets.

The drill practice was just that, a practice. It was used to tighten things up and make the movements clean. Corporal Willows drilled them the rest of the day and once back at the barracks they were given the extra duties promised in the morning. Willows had them shoveling the sidewalks outside of the barracks and polishing the brass fire stations in the barracks.

It took the better part of the evening to get the barracks back together and everybody's lockers set right. Many of the recruits went over to Grassely's bed space and inspected his work to be sure there had been no shortcuts.

Everyone was up early on Thursday; it was picture day and they would be getting their pictures taken right after lunch. The rat pack made sure their areas were perfect in every way and once again checked Grassely's area. Corporal Miller would be checking to see that their uniforms were ready and their collar dogs (pins on the collars of their tunics) were facing in the right direction.

Tony's collar dogs were eagles because he was in the Air Force. Sometimes a recruit would put them on and the eagles' heads would be facing in, not out like they should be. While this was going on, Corporal Willows was out of sight, inspecting the cleaning stations when an evil curse was heard all over the barracks "animals, you're all god-damn animals!" He called Corporal Miller telling him to join him in the washroom area and bring the recruit whose duty it was to clean the toilets.

Miller showed up with a terrified recruit named Black in tow who had no idea what was going on. "You did a shitty job in here recruit! I mean shitty! Get over here and tell me what you see Black!"

The recruit moved forward and peered into the toilet bowl. He couldn't believe his eyes because there, staring back at him was the biggest turd he had ever seen. Its mass was epic and far too big to go down the drain.

"Well, what do you see, recruit?" Willows growled. "It's the god-damned Hindenburg, Corporal," he replied as he shook his head. "Do you know how it got there, Black? Do you have any idea at all?" Black looked up at him and said "someone must have launched that baby, but his ass must be some sore. The place was spotless before we went to breakfast, so someone must have gotten back early and left this monster where he dropped it."

The Corporal ordered Black to somehow get the turd down the hole after breaking it up. Willows came out of the washroom and stood in the middle of the floor. "You heathens are real lucky that it's freezing outside or you'd be digging latrines instead of leaving that turd behind in my clean shitters."

The inspection ended and the instructors went back to the office. When they were out of sight, Black sounded off. "One of you bastards is going to pay for that, I promise."

The morning gym class consisted of more track running, like four man track relays and strength moves like rope climbing and weights. The ten mile march would be the following week and the guys were ready as long as the weather held.

Black was going around the floor asking guys if they had seen anyone around the shitters just before inspection but no one had seen anything and the guilty party wasn't volunteering an apology. Black's extra duties were fire picket that weekend, so he would not be hitting the Green and Gold and he was pissed.

The classroom found the recruits learning more and more about how to read a map and use a compass on a map to find direction and distance. They were given paper questions, a map and compass and were told they would use them again on the Grandville Ferry exercise.

Tony took to the map and compass exercise with ease. He loved figuring out locations and applying it to a map. All in all it was an easy morning for the guys and it was about to get easier because after lunch the recruits would be bused to the Hall to have their pictures taken and bused back to barracks. This was to keep their uniforms as clean as possible in the harsh weather.

In the Hall the recruits were having their individual pictures taken next to a wagon wheel. The process moved along quickly and Steve's turn was coming up. He was getting some makeup applied to his rather dark and large hickey. It wasn't the greatest job in the world, but it passed the camera test as it looked like shading.

The group shots looked great and the "Red Squad" was impressive.

The bus ride back to the barracks was strangely quiet and once there the instructors had the recruits dress in their coveralls and had them practice weapons strip and assembly, blindfolded under time for a large free pizza from a shop called "The Hollow Spot".

Everyone was keen on winning the pie so the competition was fierce amongst the Squad. The recruits were really fast and in short order they were down to two players, Stan Welding and Tony. The instructors yelled "start!" Since the recruits already had their blindfolds on, it was a matter of bending down, breaking the weapons down, and putting them back together again.

Welding was fast, but Tony beat him by two seconds. Miller declared Tony the winner and handed him the free pizza coupon. Everyone in the rat pack cheered and the recruits were on their own for the rest of the evening.

There was lots of talk in the TV room that evening about the next week and the upcoming exercises, the 10 Miler and the PT Test. The funniest thing that the guys heard right after lights out was Black calling out in the dark "I'll give twenty bucks to anyone who tells me who shit in my toilet".

Friday morning everyone was ready for the weekend and more so for Friday night. The day would be interesting because for most of it the recruits would be outside on a map and compass exercise.

The day started as always, in the gym which was a blur and before they knew it the Squad was outside in the Nova Scotia morning broken into four groups and well into their map exercise. This exercise would take them around the Base and Bayside looking for markers that they would get from questions in the exercise by azimuth and degree. The time was theirs but they had to complete the exercise before day's end. Lunch would be served in the classroom and they could stop for meals or coffee as needed.

They were to find twenty locations on their maps and mark them showing where they were. It was a cold day, but the recruits were in cold weather gear, complete with white outer wind pants and the warmest footwear they ever had called "mukluks". Tony thought they looked like big warm slippers.

The Squad was moving through the exercise confidently finding churches, radio towers and crossroads along with street signs and the main gate.

Tony and the guys loved the chance to get outside but they quickly realized that being out on the Base in the open meant they had to watch for officers. This meant paying compliments as they passed by or drove by in black cars with flags on them.

The guys had a great hay box lunch in the classroom which consisted of pork chops and gravy, mashed potatoes and peas, hot biscuits, coffee and a piece of apple pie. They all agreed it didn't get any better than this.

The rest of the afternoon went really well. Tony and his team completed the exercise with a half hour to spare so they helped clean out the classroom for the weekend.

They marched back to the barracks and saw that the hut had passed another inspection so it was time to shower, clean up and order that free pizza before heading to the Green and Gold and all that cold beer that was waiting for them.

They went to the office area and ordered two large pies from The Hollow Spot. One was all meat and the other was Hawaiian. One recruit went down to the CANEX and bought pop while the others waited for the free pie. It took quite a while but the delivery guy showed up and the free food was taken into the TV room. The boxes were opened together and words like "what the hell is that?" and "is that peaches?" could be heard.

The all-meat pizza was a greasy mess and mostly what they thought was hamburger, but the real winner was the Hawaiian pizza. Not only was it a pool of grease, but also a crazy person must have put it together. There was ham, pineapple, peaches and maraschino cherries adorning the whole thing. To top it off, there was a dough ball in the middle of the pizza where the plastic table was supposed to be!

The pizza looked really bad, but the dough ball made it look even worse. "Where's the plastic table to hold the box from crushing the pizza?" Steve said. "That's what the dough ball does," said Fanning. "Don't you know anything about East Coast pizza?"

"Out West we use a plastic table to get this done, not a nasty piece of dough, you East Coast heathen."

This brought on a lot more discussion, but they all agreed that this was not a Hawaiian pizza and The Hollow Spot would be avoided for the rest of the course.

They shared the meat pizza after patting it down with napkins to get most of the grease. They then dressed and hit the bar.

They would later find out that pizza wasn't the only thing that the Hollow Spot was known for. It seemed that they dealt drugs by hiding them under the greasy mess until they were eventually found out by the MPs!

They found a table and settled in for many beers and conversation about the map and compass exercise.

It had been a good week and Tony and the pack were keenly aware of the next couple of weeks which would lead to their graduation. Everything from now on would be done outside and the time would even go quicker.

They ate lots of bar snacks like popcorn, and nasty little pepperonis that came in a vacuum bag that got tastier as the night moved on. It was the little cans of cocktail wieners, or Vienna sausages that were the biggest hit. You take them out of the can, put them in a bowl, pour barbecue sauce on them and put them in the microwave for a couple of minutes. The guys wolfed them down.

Tony liked sitting around the table talking to these guys. They had become quite a close knit group over the past weeks and going out into the bush with them would be a blast. The talk got around to their weapons and had anyone ever fired anything like them before.

Everyone agreed that firing the FNC-1 was going to be an experience that would last them forever. Many 10-Penny and Moosehead beers went downrange and the group headed back to the barracks just as hungry as before. A quick call brought the delivery guy back again, but this time he was bearing hamburgers and chicken.

Sleeping in was good for the soul and the guys took full advantage of the fact that it was the weekend. More beers Saturday night and more down time Sunday morning got the group ready for week eight.

Chapter 29

The pack knew that week eight would be the start of their practical testing, leading into major exercises and then graduation. Their hearts pounded heavily at the thought.

Monday morning Corporal Dane reminded them of their test the next day on pushups and sit-ups. Each recruit had to complete the exercises in order to fulfill the physical requirements of their training plan. Tony knew he had it in the bag. He also liked running on the track. It gave him an opportunity to be with his thoughts and remember what was behind him and what was ahead. For a brief second he thought about Betty. He thought about finishing the training and moving on to Lac St Denis, a radar site in Quebec where he would learn to be a radar operator and after that who knew what was in the cards for him.

The next class would be a briefing on the next couple of weeks and the practical exercises coming up. Tony was really looking forward to these. As he expected, the instructors reminded them of the GSK test that would take place Wednesday and the importance of passing the multiple choice exam or face recourse because there would be no rewrite.

Thursday would be their drill test and Friday the 10 Miler. It would be a very busy week.

The briefing that morning outlined the National Survival Training they would be getting that afternoon. It would include the role the military would play in times of National disaster. Mostly, National Survivor teams were there to help people when it was necessary. Tony and the recruits would be learning about rescue techniques and how to use ropes properly which meant knot tying or what they called lashing.

Week Nine, would begin with Exercise Granville Ferry, a two day stay in the bush, using what they learned in class would be tested. Word was going around that there wouldn't be too much sleep happening during the two days. The exercise was constructed to deprive you of sleep to see how you react.

Tony and his Squad were also told that they were going to be running what was called "the Confidence Course" on the Friday. This was in an area out in the Granville Range bush that consisted of many obstacles that they had to find their way across, under, over, climb nets, doing whatever it took to get to the end of the course while carrying their weapons, wearing their helmets and being dressed in heavy winter clothing.

Miller reminded them that most of the run would be down hill and that safety was the name of game, not coming in first. Tony reminded himself to talk to the rat pack about running the course as a group so as to help each other get through safely.

Miller also reminded the recruits about their run up Heart Break Hill that was scheduled for Monday morning of week ten.

At the end of the lecture, Corporal Miller took questions and then told them to relax and enjoy the experience. He knew that for the Air Force guys, this was a one-shot. They would probably not be involved in bush exercises again. For the Army types in the course, this was only the beginning and not near what they would be expected to do.

That afternoon, the Squad was introduced to National Survival Training and the need to be able to rescue people from dangerous situations using ropes, ladders and anything else they could find. They learned the importance of a ladder and how it could be used for tasks other than climbing. Tony didn't know it, but it made a great stretcher.

The recruits spent time learning knots, like the bowline. Tony was told that to remember how to do a knot he should use a funny little rhyme. It had something to do with a rabbit in a hole. Other knots like clove hitches, square knots and reef knots were practiced many times along with other tying techniques.

They practiced lashing recruits to a stretcher and carrying them around properly until they were proficient. This made for a very quick afternoon. The next day they would apply what they learned in an exercise disaster situation.

Tuesday morning came fast and everyone was keenly aware that the PT test was in front of them. Corporal Dane had them form two lines in the middle of the floor. Half of them were on their backs and the other half held the feet of the guys on the floor.

On the word go, the recruits on the floors started doing sit-ups while the man holding his feet did the counting. On the 30-count they changed positions and the drill was repeated.

The pushups were even easier and the Squad counted them out in no time flat. Tony took a deep breath. The PT test was over and he could feel a sense of pride. He looked at Keith and Ron and saw them congratulating each other.

Corporal Miller's class consisted of reviewing GSK questions and practicing knots on chairs and each other. Miller knew they had passed the PT test and was happy to let the Squad relax a little, but he was watching for bad knots just the same.

Lunch consisted of constant talk about the PT test and the exercise they would be involved in that afternoon.

They were marched out to an old two-story building that was missing some windows, had no porch and the door was hanging off its hinges. They entered the main floor to be met by a damp, musty smell that grabbed their noses right away, even with the wind blowing in from the missing windows.

Corporal Willows explained that for exercise purposes, the scenario would be that the building had been badly damaged during a storm and they were to look for casualties and remove them from the area. The recruits were broken up into two groups, one being the casualties and the other group the rescuers.

They were in a large open area with no stairs to the second floor, but there were large holes in the upper floor. The recruits moved around the main floor lashing things together that looked dangerous and tied ladders to beams to use them as stairways to the second floor.

Everybody was doing something to complete the exercise. Some of the recruits were used as casualties and were transported to the open by stretcher where first aid was applied.

Tony's group was on the second floor with a casualty named Kidlark that had a broken leg and had many unknown injuries. There were no stairs to use, so the group lashed Kidlark to a ladder and lowered him down through a hole in the floor to get him to safety.

The second floor was fifteen feet to the main floor and Kidlark was having a fit at the thought of being tied to a ladder and lowered through a hole in the floor by four guys he barely knew. It turned out that Kidlark was pretty light and the procedure went without a hitch. The exercise was completed and Kidlark thanked the guys for not dropping him!

Chapter 30

Every day that week there was something going on that involved some type of testing. On Wednesday, the GSK test would be taken but the guys had been studying for a long time and knew it was going to be a slam dunk.

PT was easier since the testing was complete. Corporal Dane had the Squad competing in a floor hockey game. It was a good way to start the day leading to the GSK test.

Tony's guys lost the game but told the winners that they would play again and the storey would be different.

When they walked into the classroom for the GSK they noticed that the desks had been moved around and there was a space between each one of them. They sat down without saying a word and were told by Corporal Willows that he and Corporal Miller would be monitoring the test. They would have two hours to complete the questions and hand in their paperwork including any rough notes. Any attempt to cheat would be met with immediate discipline and probable dismissal from training.

Corporal Miller then gave the order and all eyes focused on the test papers in front of them.

Tony could hear Miller moving around behind him but he stayed focused on his task. He finished and was surprised to see he still had twenty minutes to go. He turned his paper over and lifted his head to see that some of the pack had also finished and were looking at the instructor.

Miller motioned to them to move out into the hall and not to talk. When the exam time was up they were asked to return to the classroom. The papers were gathered up by the instructors who explained that the papers would be graded and the Squad would be debriefed on the results the next day.

Lunch was a blur with discussions about the test and before they knew it, it was time for drill. It was second nature now and the time went quickly by but the test had unnerved a few and they got their asses chewed out for not concentrating.

The next day the Squad played a basket ball game and another game called around the key which made gym time stress free.

The recruits returned to the classroom and waited for the instructors. Miller went to the front of the classroom and set the test papers in front of him. "Let's get right to this," he said. "You all passed, but some only by the skin of your teeth."

You could feel the air move around the room as twenty deep breaths happened at once.

He handed out the test papers and the recruits could see their scores and where they had gone wrong. Tony scored 136 out of 150 questions and he closed his eyes to thank some unknown power for helping him through.

Corporal Willows went over some of the questions that the guys had trouble with and declared that this portion of the training was over, but the information that they learned was something they would use all their military careers. The relief of passing the GSK test was short lived because right after lunch the recruits would be heavily involved in their drill tests.

As Tony entered the Drill Hall he thought that the week was becoming a roller coaster ride of ups and downs. The drill test was under the command of Major Edwards, the School's Second in Command. Tony heard that he was a fair man, but was not afraid to fail a platoon that didn't measure up.

The Platoon was taken through standing rifle drill; movements on the march; and saluting with weapons. Then there was a general inspection by Major Edwards and Sergeant Akern.

After the drill test the Major turned the Platoon back over to the Sergeant, having a short discussion with him at the door before leaving the building.

Sergeant Akern stood the Platoon to "at ease," there was a long pause before he called them to attention and addressed them. "Ok," he said. "The Major thinks you can drill and will not embarrass the school during graduation; well done." He dismissed the Platoon and walked away.

Corporal Willows gave the Squad ten minutes to shake it off before he talked to them about the next day and the 10-Miler. The whole Squad was shaking each others' hands and slapping each others' backs knowing that it was just about over and they were still there.

"I've never been more relieved in all my born days," said Fanning. "I damn near tripped," Van Meter said, "and I thought he saw me." Tony piped in "tomorrow, I'm going to drink Moosehead beer until I grow antlers."

Corporal Willows told them to crowd around. He was going to explain the next day's march. It would be full-pack, webbing, helmets and weapons. He told them to carry water because it would be a long afternoon. Most of all, he told them to relax and to let it happen.

The Squad was then dismissed and they marched back to the barracks and to the Mess Hall to talk about the drill test and the next day's march.

In the blink of an eye they woke to Friday morning. Corporal Dane was never at a loss for giving them something to do during gym. This time it was volleyball. Tony's team won and they took a victory lap around the gym holding the ball. He had to admit that he was having a pretty good time.

Corporal Willows was a wealth of information when it came to long marches. He had been hard Army for over twenty years and was a veteran when it came to the long march. "Nothing loose" was the first order of business. "Don't have anything bouncing around, there's nothing like having your bayonet scabbard hitting you in one spot for ten miles to drive you crazy. Make sure your boots are snug, but not too tight."

The recruits had plenty of questions, like "what if you have to pee, or worse?" This brought a few chuckles from the class. The whole thing ended up with Willows telling them to relax, take a breath and just go with it.

The recruits had a light lunch and found themselves out on the Granville Range Road preparing to take on the 10-Miler. The Range Road was used to transport recruits out to the shooting ranges and the confidence course. It was surrounded by deep woods and rolling hills.

Tony thought it was a really nice area and could picture himself running there in the next weeks.

Corporal Willows took the lead and Miller was in the rear, watching for stragglers. The command was given to move out and the recruits stepped forward with determination.

The guys were talking quietly to themselves and giving words of encouragement to each other. Tony was in his head, and heard little of what was going on around him. He kept taking mental notes as to what his body was doing and how he was feeling. They marched on and on and every now and then, Willows would set a stronger pace and the recruits would find themselves doubling down the road for a mile or two.

The afternoon rolled on and the miles clicked off. Between marching and running the Platoon was holding up rather well but Tony was starting to notice that his feet were getting sore and his ankle was letting him know that the end was near. Time moved on and Tony was starting to panic when Willows called out "one more mile One Platoon!"

Tony prayed that Willows wasn't going to have them run that last distance. They were coming up on the corner they had started from and Tony knew he was going to complete the run.

Willows called a Halt and the recruits started to cheer and congratulate each other. It had been a hell of a march and a hell of a week!

One more surprise was waiting for them as they formed up to march back to the barracks. Corporal Willows had laid on transport for them so they weren't walking home!

Long showers later the guys were sitting in the TV room talking about the march and the week. Everyone agreed that week eight was the hardest one of all thus far.

The guys were still pretty tired from the march, so getting dressed just to go to the Mess Hall was out of the question. They ordered a bunch of chicken and chips and relaxed until it was time to go to the bar and toast the Squad and try to drink all the Moosehead the bar had.

Tony's ankle was still sore but a few beers and some ice was doing the trick. Saturday night was pretty much the same. This time the pack went down to the CANEX to look around and have a burger or two. Sunday was for sleeping in and spending time checking their gear to be sure that nothing was left behind that might be needed in the bush, most importantly, an extra pair of heavy socks.

Chapter 31

The Squad was up early Monday to start week nine. The excitement of what was coming kept them from getting too much sleep. Exercise Granville Ferry would be conducted on Monday and Tuesday over a 48 hour period and then on Friday of that week the Platoon would run the Confidence Course and walk the shooting ranges to get ready for weapons qualifications.

The trucks pulled up to the barracks at 0800 hours and the Platoon loaded their gear into the back and climbed aboard. The drive to Granville Range was a short one but the march into the woods, carrying all of their equipment took over an hour. Corporals Willows and Miller were leading the way and before long called a halt. They explained that this area would be the recruits' home for the next two days and nights. They would be getting little sleep if any during the time there.

They set up a main camp area, complete with sentries that would be rotated every six hours during the next two days.

Water stations, fire pits, first aid tents and latrines were dug into the frozen earth. They had packed some food but mainly they would be eating ration packs which would be a new experience for everyone.

The instructors showed the recruits how to build hooches in the snow, which were basically lean-to's that were insulated from the weather by fir tree branches and rain ponchos to keep them warm and dry.

The guys spread out and found areas not too far from the main camp to build their "nests" and spent several hours on them, making sure they would be warm for the night. One thing was for sure, Tony thought, the Canadian Forces winter clothing and sleeping bags were the best in the world.

Lunch was what they brought in, mainly bread and peanut butter, crackers and cheese. The Platoon was broken into four Squads and Exercise Granville Ferry began.

For the next two days and nights, the Squads were required to go out on patrols, demonstrate bush crafts like starting a fire and cooking. They were asked to read maps and use a compass during the marches in the day and night and lead patrols in exercise situations.

The night compass marches were the best, Tony thought, because the guys were on their own the entire time. Some of the tough times were when they had to carry a man on a litter through the bush to a designated position in the middle of the night.

The instructors would ambush the patrols from hidden positions just to see how they would react, day and night. Tony dove for the bush to try and find cover but was shot immediately. He could hear the instructors yelling at him from somewhere. "You need more practice, recruit!"

When they did get a bit of rest, it was in a building called the "Butler Hut." This was where they ate their first ration packs. It was a new concept for the Squad. Wieners and beans, Jambalaya, cheese and crackers, powdered coffee and biscuits were on the menu. The recruits wolfed them down like they were steak and potatoes.

Everyone was kept busy for the two days and when Tony could, he'd climb into his sleeping bag with his weapon and fall fast asleep.

The days went quickly and Tony had a great time. Wednesday night found the Squad back in their barracks, washing their clothes, and polishing their boots. Thursday was more of the same.

Friday morning started out sunny, with a bit of wind coming off the Bay. It was minus 10, but to Tony it was a perfect day. They were on their way to the woods. The Confidence Course was located in the same wooded area as the Granville Ferry Exercise, but with a difference. The course weaved in and out of the woods on a downhill slant and was not for the faint of heart. Tony looked over at Bagley and Keith and saw them shaking their heads. "Do you believe this stuff" he said? There were culvert pipes to crawl through, rope swings, big logs to walk across, wooden walls to climb over, rope ladders to climb, and a pontoon bridge to cross. The last big obstacle was a rope bridge called "the Burma Bridge." All of this was to be done on the run with weapons, helmets and webbing.

Tony looked at Keith and said "what's the worst thing that can happen, man?" Before Keith could answer, Corporal Willows gave the order to begin and the Squad took off like men possessed.

As they moved down the hill, Miller called out "let me hear your yell, recruits!" That was answered by the whole Squad screaming their heads off as they ran down the hill into the Confidence Course.

Tony slowed his pace in order to drop down and crawl into the culvert and out the other side. Guys were jumping on ropes and swinging over ditches. Not all made the leap and had to go back and try again. The pontoon bridge was practically frozen, so the crossing was easy for all.

They had to control their pace because it was easy to fall and get hurt on the snow and ice. Getting over the wall was a team effort and the rope ladder was an icy mess. Tony had to weave in and out of the trees as he moved to this very large log that he had to run on. That wasn't happening. Tony slowed down and crawled over the icy monster. He found himself in the middle of the pack as recruits rushed by him only to pass them later on as they slipped up somewhere and found themselves on their asses.

The terrain was transitioning from down to up, and as Tony moved deeper into the woods, he looked ahead at what he knew was the Burma Bridge. It was 40 feet long and was suspended over a gorge 20 feet high. Beneath the bridge, about 10 feet down, was a catch net. The bridge wasn't really a bridge, just three strands of rope, two at the hands' high position, and one at your feet. These ropes were connected to each other by vertical strands of rope tied to the hand rails and the second strand of rope at your feet.

The task was to walk on the single strand of rope and hold the other two ropes for balance. It should have been easy, just put one foot in front of the other on the rope and move forward. Tony found that he was not alone on the bridge and the guys were stacking up behind him, and he wasn't moving as fast as they wanted him to.

This rattled Tony and he turned his head to give the guy behind him a warning. Too late, he wasn't looking and missed his footing. Tony's world turned upside down as he found himself stepping out into the open air and falling through the rope into nothing. The last thing he saw was Steve's arm extending up to grab him as he fell away.

Down he went, and panic grabbed him by the throat as he screamed. He forgot the net was below him. Everything went through Tony's mind at once and his heart was pounding fast. Suddenly, he was in the catch net, looking up at Steve with his mouth wide open. "Are you OK? Are you hurt?" "Only my pride guys, only my pride," was all he could say as he climbed out of the net and focused on Corporal Willows looking right at him from the far side of the gorge. "Are you resting Simons? Are you tired?" "No Corporal," was all he could come up with. "Get your ass back up on that bridge and cross it properly," Willows replied.

Tony climbed up on the bank and crossed the bridge, this time without any problem. The rat pack was waiting for him on the other side and when he finally got to them the calls came out "Simons, you're always showing off! You're buying the beers tonight, because thanks to you we'll be the last to finish!"

They finally walked off of the Confidence Course and marched down to the ranges to take a quick look. It was a vast flat range of land of at least 200 yards across and 800 yards long. There was a long row of firing pits and if you looked down-range, you could see target circles and figurines at different distances. There was a tower behind the pits and a walking area for the Range Officer to call commands while the Corporals watched for problems.

All the guys were smiling; this was going to be great.

That night the barracks were abuzz with congratulations and shouts could be heard "we're almost done!"

Beer that night went down fast and smooth. Tony paid his beer debt to the pack and took all the ribbing he was getting for falling off the bridge. A couple of whiskey shots later and a few more Moosehead, allowed the guys to settle down and think ahead to the next week and graduation.

They thought of where they were heading and what was in store for them. They also thought of the fact that the rat pack would be breaking up soon. Fanning AKA, Mr. Handsome, because he was Army, would be heading in another direction after graduation and they all agreed that he would be missed. Since he lost his bar card on the very first weekend, he wasn't there to celebrate but they toasted Mr. Handsome anyway and then headed back to barracks.

As they marched in the dim of the street light somebody said "does anyone remember when the instructors stopped yelling at us?"

The weekend was just like the last, beers, burgers and sleeping in. This was freedom time for the guys.

Chapter 32

Monday morning rolled in quickly. Tony woke to the realization that this was the last week, week ten. By Friday he would have graduated and would be put into holding. Holding is where a graduate went to wait until their trades' training began at another Base. After this week Tony would be known as "Private Simons," something he wanted very badly.

It was once again time for the Platoon to get into gear. Heartbreak Hill was next on the schedule and the Platoon had yet to see this monster. They had heard stories in the bar about it being 6000 feet high with a grade of about 30%. Others said that it was like a sheer rock-face climb that would take them all day. Tony and the pack knew that this was just bullshit, but it made them think about what they would be doing.

They marched out in the early morning and headed for the Granville training area, only this time they took a different road and after a half an hour, they found themselves looking at the monster they had heard so much about.

It wasn't 6000 feet or a sheer rock-face, but it looked formidable. There was a constant rise in elevation for about 200 yards at about a 35 degree grade leading to a ridge and a tree line.

The problem, Tony could see, was that it was snow-covered; which made it dangerous.

"Let's go One Platoon, show me what you've got!" Willows yelled.

They all screamed out their battle cries and attacked the hill with full-out determination. Easy at first, but with every step forward, Tony could feel a little of the energy zapped from his legs. He slowed his advance as the others ran by him, but he knew that this hill was going to humble even the strongest of them before they made it to the top.

He lost his footing many times and found himself on his knees more than once. His breathing was laboured, but he pushed on, even passing guys that ran by him earlier. He never knew his legs could be that heavy or hurt so much, but as he crested the top of the hill; he ran past Corporal Willows before coming to a stop and taking a deep breath.

Willows was growling at others that were still making the climb and swearing at the ones that were taking breaks before reaching the top.

"That was a hell of a way to spend Monday morning," Steve said. Tony agreed; he only wanted to make that climb once.

The only thing left in the day was drill. It was the one constant in Tony's life, drill. Their legs were still aching from the morning climb, but this was the last period of the day and the instructors took pity on them and made it easy.

Tuesday and Wednesday was scheduled for Weapons, Live Fire at the Ranges of Granville.

Tuesday started out overcast, cool and damp but the Platoon was eager to fire the sub-machine gun or what was known as "The Plumber's Nightmare." They were on the 25 yard range that morning because this weapon was only effective at short-range.

The recruits were first given a refresher on the handling of the weapon including loading, firing and how the weapon would react. They were reminded of safety procedures in case of emergencies.

The Squads were broken down into groups of 10 and the men picked up their SMG's and magazines and moved to the firing line. The command was given to load and the recruits inserted the magazine and cocked the weapon.

Miller yelled "fire!" and the 10 Sterlings opened fire in unison, chewing the targets in front of them and kicking up the dirt.

Tony felt a huge rush of adrenalin as his weapon came to life and destroyed the target in front of him.

The morning moved on and more recruits were given the opportunity to experience the weapon. No one expected anything to go wrong, but that's usually when it happens.

The sixth round of recruits came to the line and waited for the command to be given. Stan Welding was in this group. He got into position and wasn't sure how much the SMG would kick. The command was given and Welding cocked the weapon. The fire order was given and Stan leaned in even more before he pulled the trigger. The weapon moved slightly and Stan over-compensated, slipping back on the wet ground, weapon pointed in the air on full automatic. He turned slightly with his finger still on the trigger and the bullets sprayed the top of the firing pit until the magazine was empty and the instructor moved in and grabbed the weapon from his hands.

Everybody hit the dirt and covered their heads until the instructor called "all clear!"

Tony's life flashed before him in a few seconds.

The instructor stopped the training exercise. He then called for a 10-minute break so everyone could calm down and shake-off the nervousness. Then he put Welding right back on the line to complete his training. This time everybody stood behind the wall.

The cleaning of the weapons took the rest of the morning and after turning the weapons back to the instructors, they had to give an Ammo Declaration. This consisted of telling the instructors that they had no live rounds or empty casings in their possession.

The march back to the barracks was needed to shake out the tense muscles and to get the Squad thinking about the next day and the FNC-1.

The entire Platoon was on drill practice for the final time that afternoon. They marched around the Hall like they would be doing at their graduation. The Sergeant was in the Base Commander's position and the Platoon practiced paying compliments and saluting on the march. At the end of the practice Tony knew he was ready.

Back at the barracks everyone was talking about Welding trying to kill them all earlier and threatened to kick his ass if he didn't get his shit together for the next day.

The rat pack ordered in and spent the rest of the evening stripping and cleaning their rifles in anticipation of actually firing them on the big range in the morning. Lights out came quick and the morning even quicker. It was range day and the completion of formal training.

The Platoon marched down to the Granville Ranges and received a briefing from the range officer as to what would be happening. Basically, the recruit would move to the firing pit with his weapon, enter and wait for the order to load. The order given, magazines full of 7.62mm ammunition would be locked into the rifle and the recruit would cock the rifle and release the breach block forward. On the command "fire" safeties would be clicked off and the recruit would send rounds down range aiming at targets 100 yards away.

Tony was in the first relay and climbed into his pit, nerves tingling. The load order was given and Tony set the rifle next to his cheek and tucked it in, waiting for the recoil. He barely heard the fire command but with safety off, he began firing his FN. It was loud and kicked like a mule. Tony loved the sound of the weapon and the smell of gunpowder in his nose. He could picture his round screaming downrange, hitting his target dead in the centre. More and more rounds were fired. Brass was flying in the air as it was ejected from the rifle.

Tony knew at once that this was what he was meant to do.

There were a lot of recruits to put through and Tony's time went far too quickly. He removed the magazine from his rifle and showed the RSO (Range Safety Officer) that his mags were empty before he was cleared to leave the pit.

The morning moved quickly along and most of the recruits had fired. Two more groups of 10 were left to shoot and Tony recognized an old friend in the far pit. Mr. Football was in his pit, ready to go.

Nothing looked out of the ordinary, but then again, no one was aware that when Mr. Football stripped his weapon the night before to clean it, he put it back together with the safety sears in backwards. This is easy to do because they look the same on both ends with only a slight difference. Mr. Football had not seen the difference when he put his weapon back together again. When the order was given to fire he pulled his trigger and the weapon went full-automatic and sent the entire magazine round down range in under a second. The recoil pulled the weapon up and to the side.

The Safety Officer was in the pit in less than a second, gripping the weapon, pinning it to the ground and putting it on "safe." Firing on the range was held up for many hours as the safety team was called in and went over Mr. Football's weapon looking for the problem. The problem was identified and Mr. Football was given shit up one side and down the other for bringing a dangerous weapon on the range. He was lead away in handcuffs and not seen again.

With the firing completed, it was time to clean the brass off the firing lines and check for live rounds. The recruits were then marched back to the barracks.

Everyone was thinking about what they had just been through and what was still to come – Graduation! It was only Wednesday but the recruits knew that at the end of the week they would be graduating.

The weapons definitely needed to be cleaned after a day on the ranges, so the entire barracks stripped their FNs and cleaned them until they gleamed. The next day, during the morning inspection the recruits were told that they would be returning their combat clothing to stores and wearing work dress for the final day of the course.

They had to clean their combats and gather together their webbing, and winter gear. They were told to blacken their combat boots, tie their laces together, and put everything in their barrack boxes to be ready for Friday morning.

Cleaning and packing took most of Thursday and everyone agreed it seemed strange to be back in work dress.

Friday morning the recruits found that a bus had been laid on for them and before he knew it, Tony was standing in front of the stores' clerk returning his gear and getting his civilian clothes back before climbing back on the bus.

Back in the barracks he noticed right away how empty his bed space looked and now the place had a hollow feeling about it. Corporal Willows briefed them on Travel Orders, tickets and schedules and everything they would need to get them to their new Bases. They were told that the majority of the recruits would be leaving right away after graduation and some would have to wait.

Training was over and the only thing left to do was to graduate. Corporal Willows went through what it would look like and the mass of people that would be there to watch them. Tony knew that this was something he would experience only once in his life time!

Corporal Miller came into the barracks with several large boxes and when he opened them up, they revealed white belts with shiny brass buckles, white gloves, scabbards, rifle-straps and silver bayonets.

Chapter 33

The bus arrived at 1300 hours and transported the course to the Drill Hall they knew so well but this time it was packed to the walls with all the other in-house courses, Officers and Platoon Commanders. Flags were unfurled and moved in the wind when a door was opened.

Tony was standing behind a seating area, waiting for the rest of the Squad, checking himself over when out of the corner of his eye he could see a recruit who he did not know walk over and stop in front of him. The recruit looked at Tony in his parade dress uniform and white belt.

"Can I ask you a question, Graduate?" he asked. I didn't mean to interrupt you on your day but I have to ask. Tony looked at him quizzically, "what is it Recruit Pool?" Tony asked. "Look at me," Pool said. "Really look at me. Do you think I can be where you are in a couple of months? It's hard here," he said, "really hard." Tony looked at him and saw himself a long time ago. "Do you have a friend here, Pool?"

Tony asked. "Yes I do," was Pool's response. Tony looked hard at him and told him to go to his friend and make a pact that they would have each other's back for as long as they were here.

Tony then left the recruit where he was and moved to where his Platoon was forming up, right in front of the main dais.

The Sergeant called them to attention as the Base Commander arrived. A few awards were handed out to recruits that excelled in one area or another.

The band started to play and the Sergeant gave the order to march. Away they went. Tony was never prouder of himself for what he had accomplished. They marched around the Hall with everyone watching and stopped in front of the Base Commander. The order was given to salute the Base Commander with rifles. Tony knew that it was executed to perfection.

The Base Commander made a small speech and thanked them all for being there. Then looking at the Platoon, he said "Graduating Course 7247, you are dismissed, and well-done!"

It was over before they knew it and back on the bus the guys were going crazy congratulating each other. Corporal

Miller collected all the whites and bayonets to make sure nothing was missing.

Tony sat next to Keith on the ride back to the barracks and looking at his friend he said "it's been awhile since the train station, buddy." "Feels like forever, Tony, and it's only just beginning."

They sat silent for awhile and Tony told Keith that he probably would not have made it if it were not for his friendship. Keith glanced over at Tony and said "you talk too much, man."

Chapter 34

There was only one more thing to do, the weapons would be returned. Tony hated the thought of handing in his rifle, but he was sure he'd see one again. "Any problems with this weapon, Private?" the clerk asked. "Not a one, Corporal," Tony said as he handed it over. Tony turned and walked away.

The rest of the day was barracks cleanup, top to bottom. Willows and Miller wanted the place to be as clean as they had received it. Before the instructors left the barracks, they reminded the Squad that the next day the main body of the course would be moving out as per their Travel Orders and the remainder would be in holding until it was time for them to go.

Saturday came really fast. Bright and early the recruits were saying goodbye to each other and promising to get together down the line. The buses rolled up and the recruits piled in.

Ken Fanning was the last to board. He said his goodbyes the night before but wanted to shake Tony's hand one more time. "Take care Mr. Handsome," Tony said, "and keep your head down and stay alive." Ken smiled, turned away and was gone.

Within the hour another bus rolled up and the remainder of the course piled in and headed for the holding block. The remaining seven recruits were dropped off at holding which was just another barracks, only a little older. This place was used to house men for short periods of time. The Corporal in the main office issued them bedding and reminded them, even though they were not in training, they were in the military and should act accordingly.

They would be in holding a week. "I need something to eat and a lot of beer," said Keith as he headed for the door. The rest agreed and before long they had eaten large steaks and were looking for beer. There were seven of them left, but losing Fanning was strange. They toasted him a time or two and laughed at some of the weird shit he got himself into. Each guy had his own story to tell.

Van Meter was laughing with the rest but he seemed to be laughing at himself also. Keith spotted this and yelled at him across the table. "Well, are you going to tell us what you're cracking up about?" Van Meter broke out laughing again. "It was me guys, I'm so sorry, but it was me. I left that monster turd in the toilet that morning and was too scared to own up to it. I flushed, but it didn't go down." The table broke out laughing at the thought of Black running around looking for the bastard that left it for the Corporal to find. "That deserves another toast," Steve said, and raised his glass high. "To the Hindenburg!" he said. The whole table lost it again and the good times continued right to closing.

It was Moosehead Mania at the Green and Gold that weekend. It was time to celebrate the long journey to get here. Many stories were told that weekend but one thing they all agreed on. They would have never made it here if they hadn't pulled together.

Chapter 35

Base holding isn't what it's cracked up to be. Contrary to popular belief, you don't just sit around, eating and drinking beer until it's time for you to leave. You're free labour! You get tasked with all kinds of shitty little jobs and if you still need to get any medical stuff done, now is the time.

Most of the rat pack had dental issues and being in holding was the time to get it corrected. It went on for hours and hours. Keith had called it right when he said "we were just training aids." The worst part of dental for Tony was the fact that some recruits from the course that were also in holding, were tasked with working for the dentist. They would stand there, looking in your mouth while this tooth butcher pretended to know what he was doing.

They were at the RSM's (Regimental Sergeant Major) call at all times. One of Tony's little fun things to do was to make the RSM's coffee every morning. "Don't put the coffee grounds in before 0500 hours," he'd say. Another duty was working in the kitchen. He didn't peel potatoes though, that job was left for the civvies.

Keith's job was to assist the instructors setting up the barracks for the next course.

Tony was getting tired of Mess Hall food and decided something different was in order after a week of dental and RSM tasks. It was the Saturday night before they would move onto Trade School and he had talked to Keith earlier about getting lobster at the Red Cove Inn, just a few miles down the road. The other guys were doing their own thing and this, Tony thought, would be the best opportunity for him to tell Keith about what he'd been asking about for the past 12 weeks.

The Inn wasn't very big, but it had a spectacular view of the Bay. They ordered a couple of beers and Tony lit up a cigarette and took a big drag. Keith looked at him square on and said "well, are you going to tell me about yourself or do I have to guess? Nobody knows anything about you, Tony. I don't know anything about you either and I'm supposed to be your best friend."

Tony took a big pull on his beer and sat back. "I didn't want to talk about my past because I didn't want to be judged by the guys in the Squad. I wanted them to see me, Tony Simons, not what I used to be."

Keith was staring at him intently, not saying a word.

Tony began "I made some mistakes growing up. I grew up hard in the streets, trying to survive and make my way. Along the way I hurt people and I wasn't sorry about it. I ended up with my best friend, Mark. You saw him on the train platform that day you and I met. We joined a motorcycle gang called Lucifer's Army. I ran with them for a couple of years. Young as I was, I could hold my own and they treated me like the family I didn't have." He went on to tell Keith about the bike wars he had been involved in and that people had died because of it. He told Keith about Betty and the picture that she had given him. He told him about the blood he saw, being with the gang and that terrible look on the children's faces that morning.

Finally, he told Keith how he'd come to be on the platform that cool morning, his grandfather's memories of the army and deciding to change his life. He told Keith he didn't need the rest of the rat pack to know his story. They wouldn't understand, but he had decided that he wanted his new best friend to know. He wasn't that dark biker anymore, he was just Private Tony Simons, Canadian Military and that's how he wanted people to know him from then on.

Tony took another drag on his cigarette, sat back and looked at Keith. He could see his friend was processing all that he had just learned and was waiting for his response. Keith looked out on the bay and then back at Tony. He nodded his head, reached across the table and shook Tony's hand. Private Tony Simons, that's good enough for me.

A few more beers and a lobster dinner later, Tony and Keith went back to the barracks. Monday would be their last day in Cornwallis and the guys were ready.

The bus would pick them up at 1600 hours and would drop them off two hours later in Halifax. According to their Travel Orders, they would then fly to Montreal and then bus again for one hour to Lac St Denis, a radar site in Northern Quebec for Trades Training. They would eventually be posted to their own radar site anywhere in Canada.

Chapter 36

It sounded simple to Tony and the rest of the pack, a couple hours travel and they'd be there. They boarded the bus at the barracks and moved slowly to the gate, passing through it gave Tony a great sense of pride but he didn't look back. It was time to look forward. He could hear the course song playing over and over in his head, "You're So Vain" by Carly Simon.

Two hours later, the boys unloaded in front of the Halifax Airport and proceeded to check in only to find that their plane was delayed for an hour because of weather. They headed for the restaurant and a couple of beers and burgers later they were on their flight, on their way to Montreal International Airport. There they would meet the driver that would take them to Lac St. Denis.

The flight was only an hour, but they were already an hour late. The guys were moving quickly through the airport, heading for "Baggage Arrivals" which meant they had to go down the escalator to where the bags were off-loaded. They were having a pretty good time, joking around and whistling at the pretty girls that came up the escalator and not really looking in front of them. They missed the fact that there was a large demonstration of angry University students carrying signs that read "no more Trudeau Tyranny! Free Quebec, Independent Quebec and FLQ Quebec."

They were swarming around what looked like two Politicians that were trying to get their luggage and leave, but they were surrounded and the security guards were out-numbered.

The recruits moved closer to their carousel and were immediately recognized by the crowd as Canadian Military coming to the aid of the government officials. The crowd started yelling at the recruits in French and abandoned the two officials to concentrate on the recruits.

Tony couldn't understand what they were saying, but he did see the look in their eyes and could feel the tension in the air. He had been in situations like this before and they didn't end well. The rest of the recruits from the plane, who were heading in different directions, had not gotten there yet so it was just Tony and the rat pack. He tried to explain to them that they were just there to get their bags but the crowd was having no part of it.

They moved in closer, yelling and waving their fists in the air. Tony was sure they were swearing at him and the other guys, but he didn't understand why, until a heavy-set bearded guy in glasses spit on Tony's uniform and tried to hit him with his sign. Two other protestors were moving in, along with the bearded guy but Tony was already reacting to the situation. He had been here before.

He was back at the bike war with the Lords. He grabbed for a weapon to defend himself. Tony blinked back, just in time to see the bearded guy's sign coming down on his head. He raised his arm to block the blow, grabbed the sign and broke it in half. Tony was going to beat the man with his own sign, but decided against it. He threw the piece of wood down and moved toward the man, striking him in the face with his right fist. He went down hard and didn't get up.

This backed the crowd up a minute but Ron and Keith were still dealing with their own trouble. They were on the ground, rolling around with two heavy-set angry men. One of them tried to punch Ron in the head, but he moved to the side and the punch slammed hard into the floor breaking the man's hand. You could hear the bones break. Ron smashed his elbow into the man's face and he was done.

Keith had kneed his man in the stomach and he went down to the ground gasping for air. The rest of the recruits from the flight showed up moments later and the angry crowd faded into the airport. They wanted no part of a gang of angry servicemen.

Steve was picking Ron up off the floor and straightening his uniform. "What the hell was all that about?" he said. Ron looked up at him and said "I have no damn idea."

The guys were in the middle of sorting things out and getting their luggage and didn't see the old Corporal come up to them and step into their midst. Keith and Ron saw him first and came to a rigid attention. The Corporal looked at the recruits in front of him and said "relax guys, we don't' do that shit here. My name is Ernie; I'm your bus driver. Welcome to Quebec. I see you've already met the locals."

Tony and the guys piled into the bus, all talking at once about what had just happened.

Chapter 37

It was late, around 2100 hours and there was still an hour of travel before they got to Lac St Denis. Ernie asked the guys if they had eaten and a choir of "no's" came from the back of the bus. Ernie then said that he would stop before they got to the site so the guys and he could eat and grab a beer.

Ron looked at Tony and said "did he say we're going to have a beer?" Tony shook his head "indeed he did buddy; indeed he did." Ernie was now the rat pack's best friend. Half an hour out of Montreal Ernie pulled the bus into what looked like a roadside Inn. The sign was in French, but Tony tried the language, "Chateau Celine. Nourriture Et Boisson." Tony asked Ernie what the sign said. He laughed, "You can get a burger and a beer here, Simons, that's all you need to know."

They spent a half hour at the bar and then pushed on to St Denis. They got in at 2300 hours and were assigned rooms in a newly renovated barrack block. This was not what Tony was used to. This was two guys to a room. Tony got paired up with a recruit named Andy Hicks and Keith's partner was a rather large native guy named "Nick Sparrow."

Ernie told the guys that one of their instructors would be by at 0700 hours to take them to the Mess Hall for Breakfast, then on to the bus to go up to the site and their classroom.

Tony had not seen anything so pretty as Lac St Denis in the morning. It was all rolling hills and dense pine trees on their way to the radar site, situated atop a small hill. The Base itself was small by most standards, but most radar sites are. It had a Headquarters Building, Mess Hall, Barrack Buildings and some PMQ's or Private Married Quarters which could be seen from the top of the hill.

Tony knew that this was to be his TQ3 or Trade Qualification Training. The instructors told them it would take five weeks to complete and upon graduation they would be posted immediately to radar sites across Canada that had openings.

Training began that morning with a tour of the radar site itself. It consisted of two Height Finder Radars and a Search Radar. These antennae were covered by three white globes which they called golf balls. The site sat on top of the hill and you could usually see them for miles.

Tony and the guys were shown where they would work. The DMCC, or Data Maintenance Control Centre, was a darkened room where Air Defense Techs would sit in front of radar screens and watch aircraft coming and going through their airspace. This was a 24 hour operation and the techs would be required to work all shifts. Another piece of equipment they were expected to learn was the switchboard which turned out to be quite a chore since no one spoke French.

The instructors here were much calmer than the men in Cornwallis. They were more interested in the guys learning the equipment and doing the right things the first time rather than yelling their faces off and threatening them.

Tony found the instructors to be very friendly and they were willing to help you out if you were having problems. You could even go up the hill in the middle of the night to get extra training from the guys already working there.

One of the most interesting things Tony learned to do was to write backwards on a Plexiglas board to track aircraft during exercises.

Tony's schedule was easy. Up at 0600 hours, no "stand by your bed" inspections, breakfast at 0700 hours, then off to the Junior Ranks' Club TV room to watch Canada AM before the bus came to take you to the site.

During the weekends the course let loose and shocked most of the people that were posted there. The guys took over the games rooms and drank from Friday after work to closing. They ate everything in the vending machines and ordered pizza if they got hungry again. It wasn't a hard stretch to say this course was wilder than most and the instructors were hearing about it from the Mess Hall to the Junior Ranks' Club.

One weekend the course decided to have a party in the barracks and sleep in the hall on a brand new carpet.

They bought enough beer to actually fill a bathtub and ordered food in all weekend so the party could continue. There was serious drinking going on and the Military Police came in more than once to calm things down. Stan Welding tried to throw a pail of water at Keith, but lost his hand-hold and the pail and the water went through Keith's bedroom window.

Once again the MP's showed up and things were quiet for awhile.

The new carpet didn't look new anymore. The guys were throwing up on it or grinding pizza into it all weekend. Somehow the carpet got ripped up from the floor in front of the washrooms and the course ended up paying for the carpet replacement.

Everyone was sitting on the floor in the hallway, still pissed and eating pizza bones when the instructors came in and broke up the party Sunday morning. The Course Commandant read the riot act to the recruits and threatened jail time or expulsion from the course if it ever happened again. So things settled down for awhile.

Chapter 38

The course was moving right along. Tony was getting a lot of time on the scopes and was getting more skilled with the height finders. The only thing that was driving him crazy was the French language thing when it came to the switchboard. He picked up a few words and phrases but long conversation was a lost cause. He got along well with the instructors and they got along with him. He really liked the training, but was looking forward to his own site.

Partying on the weekends was mandatory and the pack lead the way in terms of finding places to go and beers to try. Each of these parties started off with a course drink. It was a flaming Drambuie that Ernie served up at the Junior Ranks Club, seeing that he was the bartender.

Steve, being the animal he was, heard about a peeler bar in a small town called St. Savar which was not far from the station. The single guys, that lived in another barracks said that it was definitely worth a look because the peelers were a mother and daughter team and very good-looking.

Hearing this was like throwing a roast into a pen of starving dogs. This was going to happen the next weekend and they were finally going to wear civilian clothes again. That Friday they started off in the Junior Ranks Mess with a flaming Drambuie and a lot of rum. Two cabs and $20 later the pack and six other guys from the course were in front of where they wanted to be.

The flashing neon sign above the door said "La Taniere," which Tony found out later was "The Den." They opened the door and went down about five steps into a dimly-lit, large smoky bar with flashing lights around the bar and stage and small lamps on the tables that had seen better days.

Tony and the guys got two tables close to the stage and bar and once they found the washroom they were set for the night. A table full of beers and a big tip to the serving girls meant that they would be coming back often. It was getting onto 2100 hours and the place was filling up with locals and businessmen. The lights started flashing and the room erupted into howls and clapping. On the stage, came this very attractive, middle-aged woman named Lucy and began moving all over the stage tempting the patrons and asking them what they wanted to see.

She was slowly removing her top and taunting the men with every movement. Tony and the pack were definitely loosening up. They had not seen a half-naked woman in some time. Howling, slapping and calling her over to the tables, they tucked dollar bills into her g-string and gave her a Drambuie shot every time she came near; which she happily drank.

Tony didn't know it at the time but full nudity was not allowed in Quebec, but the top could be removed and she had it off in a heartbeat and was daring the guys to touch them as she backed away. She was getting loaded and moving more provocatively for the guys, but at the same time, she was making money for herself.

Her set was over quickly and she stumbled off the stage to disappear behind the bar. The bar was going nuts and not slowing down. The lights flashed again and out came a beautiful young woman that looked surprisingly like Lucy. Rick found out from the waitress that the young woman was indeed Lucy's daughter. Her act was amazing and she too made a lot of money from the guys. She refused to take a drink when she came near and tempted the table.

Rick was in love and had to be restrained from jumping up onto the stage. The night moved along and the pack was having a great time; a loud time. They were not aware that the locals were getting pissed off with these English-speaking short-hairs, and the girls seemed to be more interested in their tables than any other.

Things were heating up but the pack was unaware that their welcome was running out quickly. The lights flashed again and out popped Lucy, drunk as a skunk and looking to party. She moved around the stage in an unbalanced seductive state and zeroed in on the guys' table to suck up their dollar bills and drink more of anything. The top came off quickly and she draped it over Steve's head. She bounced her breasts in front of his nose and stumbled back awkwardly to avoid having Steve make contact. Laughing out loud, she moved away and reached behind herself and slapped her rump. This fired up Rick to uncontrollable heights and had to be restrained.

The room was going crazy as Lucy grabbed her g-string and began to slowly pull it down before she left the stage. This was not allowed, but she did it anyway.

The room was clapping and yelling and whistling as she disappeared. The table was going crazy and did not notice that Rick was no longer there. More beer and loud laughter saw Rick coming back to the table with a big shit-eating grin on his face. "Where were you man," Tony said, "the washroom?"

Rick looked seriously at him and said he had had business to take care of and only he could do it because "you bad-asses don't have the stones." "What do you mean? Tony said. He didn't like being told that he had no stones. Rick stood up and turned around so as not to show them his face. He moved something from his pocket and turned back to the table wearing Lucy's g-string on his head, like a badge of honour.

The table went crazy and cheers could be heard all the way down the block. Rick was a hero in everyone's eyes. They stood up to toast him and his g-string. That's when all hell broke loose. A beer glass flew across the room and smashed Tony's beer bottle from his hand. Tony looked over with hate in his eyes at the table of drunken locals that took offence to the strangers and how the peelers were spending all their time with these unwelcome English pigs. Even in their broken English, Tony knew that this wasn't going to end peacefully.

Chapter 39

The room erupted in flying glass and chairs being hurled around. The locals came at the guys en masse and were met with a body of undeniable rage and power. Steve was the first to be assaulted by a tall thin guy wielding a chair over his head. He broke it over Steve's back and was immediately taken out by two blows to the face.

The two forces of drunken bodies were kicking and stomping each other with hate in their eyes. Tony was confronted by a loud over-weight Frenchman that had on a striped t-shirt that was too small for his huge belly. Tony targeted the exposed fat and gave him a mean kick to the stomach which brought him to his knees as he started to puke.

Tony moved in to help Bagley, who was taking on two more of the attackers. He evened Bagley's odds by smashing a beer mug over the Frenchman's head, knocking him out.

The bouncers of the club were pushing the battlers to the door, hoping they could take this war outside. It worked for a moment. Keith was dragging a screaming customer out the door by his hair but was punched in the back of the head by some unknown Frenchman and went down in the snow.

Welding had a guy in a headlock and was screaming his face off about how mad he was that these drunks had spoiled his night out. He rammed the drunk's head into a parked car and the man went down with a moan and wanted no more of this crazy Englishman.

The fight was breaking up and the locals finally backed off, but they were still making menacing gestures with their hands and speaking French. Things were calming down quickly but Stan was still yelling at the group of defeated drunks and shaking his fists. He wasn't done with them yet. His rage peaked when he looked around and found the biggest boulder they had ever seen and picked it up over his head.

He walked over to a big black Cadillac that was parked in the lot and slammed the giant rock down on the hood of the car with so much force it not only crushed the hood but shattered the front glass and sent the car alarm screaming. It was time to leave! Now!

They walked quickly away from the bar with Bagley proudly waving his prize above his head and laughing his ass off. They found two cabs that were looking for late pub-crawlers, gave the drivers $25 each and headed back to the Base. They were sure that this wasn't over and the local police would be making a visit to the Base for further conversations.

Chapter 40

No truer words were spoken. Two days later Tony and the rest of the recruits were marched into the Course Commandant's office to explain what had happened.

After hearing their side of the story, the Commandant got the police to drop the charges if the guys would pay half of the damages at the bar, but Stan was on the hook for the entire repair of the black caddy.

It was agreed that the peeler bar was off limits for the remainder of the course and any other drinking would happen at the Junior Ranks' Club. However, Rick was infatuated with Lucy and he went back to The Den the following weekend only to be beaten badly and sent back to the Base as a lesson. The lesson was "the pack was not welcome there."

This turned Tony into a raving madman. He convinced Ernie to take a bus load of angry students back to the bar for payback. The MPs heard of this and blocked the bus from leaving the Base.

A week before the course was to graduate; the Base was having one of its annual exercises, practicing protecting the Base during civil unrest. This meant that the Military Police and the Base Defense Force were to guard the gates and stop anyone from entering the area.

As luck would have it, Tony and the rest of the course were tasked with being the angry civilians and were to try to enter the Base and cause unrest. Tony and the pack didn't bother with the front gate; they jumped the fences at 2000 hours and terrorized the Base and personnel for several hours.

They started off by setting off the fire alarms in the maintenance areas and moved on from there. The rest of the course stormed the main gate and began yelling and tried to climb over the wall. The MPs had parked a cruiser crosswise on the road leading up to the radar site, to stop any vehicles that might get on the Base from using this road. Unfortunately for them, they left the keys in the car and John from the pack took them and drove towards the radar site. Now the MPs couldn't get up the hill to stop him!

Tony and the rest of the course had running skirmishes with the MPs around the Base for hours, until they were finally captured and thrown in jail. There were six to a small cell and the guard didn't search them very well or he would have found a screwdriver in Ron's boot.

When the guard went to the washroom, the pack, who were in one cell together, took the door off the cell and made their way around to the back of the guardhouse with a submachine gun that the guard had left behind when he went to relieve himself.

The machine gun was loaded with blanks, but it made a hell of a racket. Tony and the pack made their way back to the fence, where they came in but before jumping over he fired off the whole magazine into the darkness, making sure the guards would not venture into the area. He left the weapon leaning on the fence. He was sure they'd find it later.

As the pack went back to the main gate to await the end of the exercise, Tony looked at Keith and said "I bet they won't let us do that again." Keith chuckled and responded "I bet you they can't wait to see this course over."

Chapter 41

The course was ending and Tony knew that he and the rest of the guys would be parting company soon and going their own ways. They had already had briefings by their instructors about where they might want to be posted and had each given the instructors a list of three possible sites they might like to be assigned to.

The site selection would be based on their final marks and top scores would guarantee first choices. The pack breezed through their written and practical exams and knew that the question they all had on their minds would be answered soon.

Wednesday morning the Course Commandant came into the classroom and sat on the corner of the desk. "I can't say that this course wasn't without its challenges or that the town of St. Savar is going to miss you. I can say, it has been damned interesting and I'm glad you all made it."

Without missing a beat he opened a large manila envelope and began reading the recruits' names and their assignments.

"Private Bagley, you're going to Mont Apica. Private Stoddard, Yorkton; Private Langford, Beaver Lodge; Private Van Meter, Moosonee; Private Simons, you're going to Kamloops; Private Welding, Goose Bay."

He continued calling names until everyone was assigned a radar site and then quickly added "you leave Friday morning, good luck."

Tony was astonished. "That's a day and a half," he said.

A blur of paperwork, packing and a few quick beers later, the pack found themselves standing quietly in the Club, waiting for Ernie to drive them to Montreal. No one was saying much.

They had been together for quite some time and today it would end. They were thinking about their postings but they were also thinking about their friends around them.

Small talk on the bus put the guys in Montreal Airport an hour later. They said goodbye to Ernie and entered the airport with a bit of trepidation. They didn't know what was going to happen to them after today.

The goodbyes came faster than expected because the pack was taking flights; some now and some later. Stan left first, then Steve. With handshakes and promises to stay in touch, they melted into the crowd of travellers.

Tony and Keith were the last to separate; Tony was leaving in an hour and Keith right then.

Keith was the first to speak. "It's been quite a ride, Pilgrim," he said. "A lot has happened since I spotted you on that train platform with your biker buddy." Tony agreed and said that knowing what he knew now, because of the experience he would not have missed it for the world. Keith nodded his head and shook Tony's hand. "See you down the trail, pard." With that he turned and was lost from site in an instant.

It took a second for Tony to realize that for the first time in quite a while he was alone. Smiling to himself, he turned and headed for his gate and the plane that would take him to a new life.

During the short wait time Tony thought back to meeting Keith on the train in Port Nichols, his twelve weeks in Cornwallis and what he had learned there and the friendships he had made. These were memories he would take with him for many years to come.

It was a beautiful day for flying with bright, sunny skies and huge white puffy clouds rolling by. The giant, shiny bird screamed down the runway, grabbing at the air, trying to climb into the sky and escape the ground. The power of the mighty engines pushed the monster forward and the people inside, back in their seats. The nose of the huge aircraft was the first to leave the ground while speed and power pushed the rest of the bird into the sky finally making a gentle turn to the left while continuing to climb and head into the sun, westbound.

Glossary

AMU	Air Movements Unit
AWOL	Absent Without Leave
CANEX	Canadian Exchange
CFB	Canadian Forces Base
DMCC	Data Maintenance Control Centre
FNC	Fabrique Nationale Carabine
GSK	General Service Knowledge
MIR	Medical Inspection Room
MP	Military Police
NBC	Nuclear, Biological, Chemical
NCO	Non-Commissioned Officer
PERI Instructor	Physical Education Requirements
PMQ	Private Married Quarter
PT	Physical Training
RSM	Regimental Sergeant Major
RSO	Range Safety Officer
SIN	Social Insurance Number

BE SURE TO READ THE FINALE TO THE TONY
SIMONS SERIES "MAN OF HONOUR"

Tony will face some of the most challenging moments
of his life and at the same time, some of the most wonderful.

The road from where he was to where he needs to be
has many twists and turns. Tony must face the unknown and
make the right decisions or anything can happen. Fate must
step into his life once more.

"The Doctor stepped back and a woman in a military
uniform leaned over him. Her name was Evans, Lieutenant
Evans. She had been gathering information about the
accident while Tony lay unconscious for the previous three
days. She began telling him about what had happened and
how lucky he was to be alive.

A transport truck had come around the bend behind him
and lost traction with his trailer. The trailer slid sideways
across the road and into the ditch while continuing to slide
down the road. He hit Tony with a powerful glancing blow
to his right side and threw him 40 feet into the tree line and
down a hill. The transport continued on its deadly path
hitting and destroying Tony's car and a tow truck at the
same time. When the truck's trailer finally came to a stop

hung up on a pile of rocks, the driver, though cut and bruised, radioed the police and limped to the tree line looking for Tony to try and help him and the tow truck driver.

Tony lay in his hospital bed trying to remember but that memory was not there. 'Now what?' he asked himself. What was he going to do now?

Lieutenant Evans looked closely at him and reminded him that he was a member of the military and the military takes care of their own."

About the Authors!

Warrant Officer, Retired, Larry Edward Crandell, CD Medal; NATO Peacekeeping Medal; Gulf War Medal with Bar; Kuwait Liberation Medal; Order of St John's Medal.

Larry completed 25 years in the Canadian Military, working first on Radar Sites, then for NORAD as an Air Defence Technician. He then worked as a Nuclear Biological Chemical Defence Technician working for NATO in Germany. He is a Veteran of the Gulf War and was there when the night skies lit up as the missiles rained down on Bagdad. Larry spent many nights during the alerts alone in his shelter, out in the desert, writing journals about his experiences and wondering what he was doing there. He completed his military career as the Standards Warrant Officer at the Nuclear School in Borden Ontario.

Once retired from the military, he spent a few years working in the Alberta Tar Sands and teaching in Fort McMurray; he retired in Saskatoon, Saskatchewan and spends his time writing with his lovely wife of 38 years, Shirley.

Born on the prairies of Saskatchewan, Shirley's career of 35 years was in administration where she took to writing Newsletters and Standing Operating Procedures; and she has always enjoyed writing. She met Larry in 1980 and travelled the world with him and daughter Kathryn. Now retired, she has the time to spend on her personal passions, writing and jewelry making. She has previously published a non-fiction book called "Through the Fog."